HEINEMANN GUID
UPPER LE

MARY WEBB

Precious Bane

Retold by Florence Bell

Illustrated by Barry Wilkinson

UPPER LEVEL

Series Editor: John Milne

The Heinemann Guided Readers provide a choice of enjoyable reading material for learners of English. The series is published at five levels – Starter, Beginner, Elementary, Intermediate and Upper. Readers at **Upper Level** are intended as an aid to students which will start them on the road to reading unsimplified books in the whole range of English literature. At the same time, the content and language of the Readers at **Upper Level** is carefully controlled with the following main features:

Information Control

As at other levels in the series, information which is vital to the development of a story is carefully presented in the text and then reinforced through the Points for Understanding section. Some background references may be unfamiliar to students, but these are explained in the text and in notes in the Glossary. Care is taken with pronoun reference.

Structure Control

Students can expect to meet those structures covered in any basic English course. Particularly difficult structures, such as complex nominal groups and embedded clauses, are used sparingly. Clauses and phrases within sentences are carefully balanced and sentence length is limited to a maximum of four clauses in nearly all cases.

Vocabulary Control

At **Upper Level**, there is a basic vocabulary of approximately 2,200 words. At the same time, students are given the opportunity to meet new words, including some simple idiomatic and figurative English usages which are clearly explained in the Glossary.

Glossary

The Glossary at the back of this book on page 88 is divided into 4 sections. A number beside a word in the text, like this [3], refers to a section of the Glossary. The words within each section are listed in alphabetical order. The page number beside a word in the Glossary refers to its first occurrence in the text.

Contents

A Note About This Story

This story is about life in the country in the west of England, about two hundred years ago. It tells the story of Prue Sarn and her brother and how they tried to find love and happiness.

The lives of country people at this time were very hard. They had few machines to help them with their work and they often died of hunger or cold while they were young.

Introduction

I am an old woman now, but I am very happy. I often sit by the fire and think of the days when I was young. I can remember very clearly. Before I die, I want to write down everything I remember.

I want to write down the truth about my family – the Sarns. People told lies about my family. I want to write down the truth. And I want to write about the Beguildys – father, mother and daughter. I want to tell how their lives were joined with ours. Many people said that Mister Beguildy was a wicked man. Perhaps he was. But the learning[1] he gave me was a blessing, not a curse[2]. It was because of my learning that I came to know Kester. But it is not yet the time to speak of Kester.

Now we live near the mountains. From my window, I can see the wide sky and the high-flying clouds. When I was young, it was different. Then I lived in the house of Sarn. There were high trees round the house. We could only see the sky reflected[4] in the waters of Sarn Mere[1].

1

A Funeral at Sarn

I begin my story in 1811. That was the year my brother Gideon Sarn was seventeen. I, Prudence Sarn, was two years younger.

Gideon was already a fully-grown young man, nearly as big as Father. They were both tall and dark. They were both strong men and quick-tempered[4] too.

Mother was a little woman who hated quarrels. Mother often

cried and she cried most when she looked at me. For I, Prue Sarn, had a hare-lip². I was marked from birth with the Devil's curse. When I was a child, it did not trouble me. But as I grew older, I saw people looking at me and whispering to each other. Then I grew sad and ashamed⁴.

One fine Sunday in June, the bells were ringing and calling the people to church. That Sunday, Father and Mother had to look after the bees and could not come with us to church. Gideon and I were sent to church, dressed in our best clothes. Always, when we returned, Father would ask us questions about the sermon⁴. If we could not answer, we would be punished.

But Gideon was not worried. He persuaded me not to go to church. Instead, we met Jancis, Wizard Beguildy's ² daughter, and played with her down by the Mere.

Jancis Beguildy was as pretty as a flower, with white skin, long, golden hair and a mouth like a rose. And although she was a wizard's child, no one called her a witch. For she did not have a hare-lip, like me.

When we got home, Father was eating his supper.

'Well, what was the sermon about?' he asked.

'Burning and hell-fire²,' Gideon answered quickly.

'And what did Parson say?'

Then Gideon made up a story that no one could believe. Father's face grew angrier and angrier. At last he shouted out, 'Liar! There was no sermon at all. Parson visited us here at Sarn. Many people were sick. No one was in church.

'You did not go to church!' Father shouted, 'and you've lied to me and tried to make a fool of me, your own father!'

Father stood up, his face angry and red. He reached for the horse-whip.

'Now I'm going to give you a beating you will never forget!'

But as Father came across the kitchen, Gideon ran at him. He hit Father hard in the stomach with his head. Father fell down heavily onto the stone floor.

Father lay on his back completely still.

Father's breathing was so loud that the sound filled the whole house. Mother loosened his clothes and poured water on his face, but it did not help Father. The awful sound went on and on. Mother cried out, 'Sarn! Sarn! Oh, Sarn, my husband!'

Mother tried to make Father drink some brandy, but his lips were tight shut. Then the sound changed. Then it stopped. There was a dreadful silence.

Gideon stood in the middle of the room. When all was quiet he said, 'He's dead, Mother. I'll go and tell the bees or they'll fly away[2].'

Mother and I sat there, crying. After a while, Gideon came back. He helped us put Father's body on a mattress[4].

'Go to bed, Mother,' Gideon said. 'I've shut up the animals and everything's safe. I told the bees. They're happy that I am master now.'

―――――

We buried Father at night. Gideon was the chief mourner[4]. He wore a tall black hat and black gloves. He carried a stick with black ribbons on it.

We put the coffin on a waggon all covered with flowers. The waggon was pulled to Sarn church by oxen[3]. The light from our burning torches was reflected in the water of Sarn Mere. As we walked behind the waggon, the church bells rang out clearly through the summer's night.

The coffin was placed on the ground on one side of the open grave. On the other side, there was a table covered with a white cloth. On the table, there was a big mug full of Mother's home-made wine. One by one, everyone came forward, drank some wine from the mug and said, 'I drink to the peace[2] of him that's gone.'

There was another small mug of wine and some bread on the table, but no one touched them.

7

Then Sexton[4] stepped forward.

'Is there a Sin Eater[2]?' he asked.

'Alas, no!' Mother cried out. 'There's no Sin Eater for poor Sarn.'

It was our custom when a man was buried for a poor man to be the Sin Eater. The poor man would be paid to drink the wine and taste the bread. When he did this, the dead man's sins became his own.

'Alas, there is no Sin Eater for my poor Sarn!' Mother cried again.

There was silence. And then a strange and terrible thing happened. Gideon stepped up to the table and said, 'There is a Sin Eater.'

'Who? I see no one,' Sexton said.

'I'll be the Sin Eater,' Gideon said. He took up the mug, looked at Mother and said, 'Will you give the farm and all to me if I am the Sin Eater, Mother?'

'No, no, Gideon!' Mother cried. 'Don't do it! Sin Eaters are cursed!'

'Then I won't drink the wine and eat the bread,' Gideon said. 'Father can keep his sins and go to Hell.'

'No, no!' Mother cried again. 'He must rest in peace. If there's no one else, you must do it!'

'And you'll give me the farm, Mother?'

'Yes, yes, my dear. I do not care about the farm,' Mother cried. 'You can take it all.'

So in front of everyone, Gideon drank the wine and ate the bread.

'Rest in peace, Father,' Gideon said. 'I take your sins on my own soul and they become mine.'

Then the coffin was put in the grave and the funeral was at an end.

After the funeral, everyone came back to Sarn for the funeral feast[4].

When we got home, Missis Beguildy had the fire burning

'Will you give the farm and all to me if I am the Sin Eater, Mother?'

brightly. She had warmed the wine and brought some more funeral cakes. So everyone had plenty to eat and drink. Missis Beguildy was a good woman. But people were afraid of her husband – he was called the Wizard of Plash.

Gideon stood in the doorway, tall and powerful. He was Master of Sarn now. Everyone could see that.

'Hay harvest starts tomorrow,' Gideon said.

'It's well after twelve, young Sarn,' said Parson. 'It's tomorrow now. I wish you well today and in all your tomorrows.'

'Tomorrow, oh tomorrow!' Jancis Beguildy said, her mouth round and red as a rose. 'Tomorrow is a word of hope, I do believe!' And she smiled across the room at Gideon.

Then all the people sang a holy song and began to leave. Mother stood by the door, giving out the funeral cakes all wrapped in black-edged paper.

The birds were singing and the sun was rising.

'It's too late for sleep now, Prue,' Gideon said to me. 'Let's go down to the orchard[3]. I want to tell you what I have planned.'

2

Promises

We sat under an old apple tree in the orchard.

'Now, Prue,' Gideon said. 'You're to listen carefully to all I say. You and me have got to work together.'

'And Mother?' I asked.

'Oh, well, Mother too. But she's old. If we two work hard together, Prue, so will she.'

'I'm not afraid of work,' I said.

'Good, because there'll be plenty of work to do,' Gideon answered. 'I want to make money, a lot of money. Then we'll sell the farm. We'll go to Lullingford and buy a big house. We'll be rich, Prue, and I'll be a powerful man. You'll have dresses, china[4], anything you like. But it'll take years and years.'

'Why can't we stay here, at Sarn?' I asked sadly. 'I don't want to live in a big house.'

Gideon's eyes shone with a cold, hard light. 'But you must live with me,' he said. 'I shall do as much as Father did, and more. I'm a strong man, Prue. And you'll always be here to help me. You will never marry.'

'Not marry, Gideon? Oh, I'm sure I'll marry. Every girl marries, don't they?' I said.

'I'm afraid no one will want to marry you, Prue,' Gideon answered.

'Not want to marry me? Why not?'

'Ask Mother,' Gideon answered. 'Maybe she can tell you why the hare crossed her path and gave you a hare-lip.

'But forget your hare-lip now, Prue,' Gideon went on. 'When we've got a lot of gold, I'll get a doctor to cure you. It'll cost a lot. So you must work hard and do as I tell you. You must swear to work hard, Prue. Swear it on the Bible. And I will too.'

So Gideon went into the house to get the Bible. I sat under the tree, very sad. I thought of the husband and baby I would never have.

Gideon came back. 'Hold the Bible in your hand, Prue,' he said.

'But what about Mother?' I asked.

'Mother?' Gideon said. 'What about Mother? The farm belongs to me now. You heard Mother say so at Father's funeral. Do you think I took Father's sins for nothing? Now say after me: I promise to obey my brother, Gideon Sarn, in all things. I promise to work for him as a servant, for no money, as long as he wants it. I'll obey him in all things. I swear it on the Holy Book. Amen.'

I repeated my brother's words. Then Gideon put his hand on the

Bible and said, 'I swear to take care of my sister, Prue Sarn. To share everything with her when we are rich. And when we've sold Sarn, I promise to give her fifty pounds, to cure her hare-lip. Amen.'

As Gideon spoke these words, I suddenly shivered.

'What's the matter?' Gideon asked. 'Go and light the fire if you're cold. We can talk while we eat. Mother's asleep. I've a lot more to tell you.'

So I went and lit the fire and got the table ready for breakfast. I put a few roses on the table. I always liked things to look pretty.

When Gideon came in from milking the cows, we sat down. He told me everything that he was planning to do.

First, I was going to learn how to make butter and cheese. Then every market-day³, Gideon would take our horse, Bendigo, to Lullingford, with two big basketsful of butter, eggs, cheese and honey.

'And you can pick some flowers,' Gideon went on. 'We can sell them too. Sometimes we'll have chickens, ducks or fish to sell. You'll see, Prue. We'll do everything ourselves and we'll make a lot of money.'

'But what a journey!' I said. 'It's thirty miles to Lullingford, there and back! All in one day!'

'When we've saved some money,' Gideon went on, not listening to me, 'we'll buy another cow. We'll buy oxen, to help us plough³. We'll keep pigs in the woods³ and Mother can look after them.

'And we'll have sheep,' Gideon continued. 'The sheep will give us wool that you and Mother can spin³. Then we can sell the yarn.

'And I shall sow corn, and grow acres³ of corn,' Gideon said. 'Corn's cheap now, but people are saying that the government is going to tax it.'

'But won't that make the corn dear?' I asked. 'Then flour will become dear and bread will become dear,' I said. 'And that will be bad.'

'Maybe that will be bad for the people,' Gideon answered. 'But it'll be good for us. We'll get a good price for our corn and we'll make a lot of money.

'And now, Prue, you must go to see Mister Beguildy at Plash,' Gideon added.

'Mister Beguildy? What for?' I asked in surprise. For I knew that Gideon, like Father, did not like the man at all.

'What for? Because he can teach you to read and write. And how to keep accounts[4] too,' Gideon replied.

I was pleased that Gideon said this. I very much wanted to learn to read and write. In those days, not every lady knew how to read and write. And very few farmers' daughters could read and write.

'If Mister Beguildy agrees to teach me, how shall I pay him?' I asked.

'You can dig his garden for him and plough his fields,' Gideon said. 'You're strong. Beguildy's a lazy man. He does nothing all day. Put on your best black clothes and go there this evening.'

Then Gideon went off to the hay-meadow[3] with his scythe, to cut the fresh hay.

That afternoon, when I finished the milking, I went upstairs and took off my working clothes. I dressed myself carefully in my best black clothes. It was not often that I had the chance to wear them. I curled my hair in long brown ringlets.

When I came downstairs Mother said, 'The ringlets are really nice, Prue. And you've got a very neat figure, child. You're getting so tall too.'

But then she started to cry.

'Was it my fault that the hare crossed my path? Was it my fault?'

'Oh Mother, Mother, don't cry. Please don't cry. Listen Mother, I don't care if I have a hare-lip or not!'

And with that I ran out of the house, crying. For I had told a lie – I did care.

As I ran through the fields, I thought about what Gideon had said. I was glad about the reading and the writing. I would learn to read and write and I would have some power over Gideon. Then later, he'd give me the fifty pounds. And the doctor's cure would make me as beautiful as a fairy[2]. Then a lover would come for me and soon I'd be married, with a baby sitting on my knee.

And so, happily, I went on to Plash. The Beguildys' stone house at Plash was half-cave and half-house.

Outside the house, I saw Jancis, her gold hair shining and her face like a white flower.

'Oh, you've got ringlets, Prue!' she said. 'I'd like to have ringlets too.'

'If you want,' I replied. But I thought Jancis was pretty enough without the ringlets.

I went into the house and called out, 'Mister Beguildy! I want you to teach me to read and write and keep accounts. I'm going to pay you by doing work for you, Gideon says. Gideon and me's going to get rich, buy a big house and . . .'

'Wait a bit,' Beguildy said. 'You've got to do the learning first. You'll do as I say, or I'll not teach you.'

Missis Beguildy looked at me in surprise.

'Will you be clever enough to do the learning, child?' she asked. Like many people, she thought that because I had something wrong with my body, I would be stupid and unable to learn anything.

'Prue's clever enough to learn,' Beguildy said. 'She'll be a good scholar. I can tell that. We'll start the learning next week, Prue.'

So I went home. I felt like a lady, walking in my best clothes. Once every week, I'd go and get learning from Wizard Beguildy. Prue Sarn would be a scholar!

Mother looked up when I went into the house. I asked her where Gideon was.

'Cutting hay by moonlight,' she said. 'He works harder than any lad I ever knew.'

So I went to the hay-meadow. Gideon had cut as much hay as a man would have done.

'Come in to supper, Gideon,' I said.

'Mister Beguildy! I want you to teach me to read and write
and keep accounts.'

'So you're back are you?' Gideon replied. 'Have you shut up the chickens[3] for the night?'

'No.'

'Be quick and do it then. It should have been done an hour ago. Have you looked at the traps[3]?' Gideon went on.

'No, I thought you would,' I answered.

'When I'm cutting hay, I've no time for anything else,' said Gideon. 'And when you've done the chickens and traps, you can set some fishing-lines[3] in the Mere. I've got some wood to cut.'

'Setting fishing-lines takes a long time and I'm no good at it,' I said, almost crying. It was late and I was tired.

'Did you make a promise to work hard, or didn't you?'

'I did, Gideon. Yes, I did.'

'Then keep it.'

I did all the things Gideon told me to. But I cried as I did them. I wished there was an easier way of curing my lip and making me as beautiful as a fairy.

So the hard times started. But I was learning to read and to write. When I felt unhappy, I went up to the attic[4]. I could sit quietly in the attic far away from Gideon and the work of the farm.

Sitting between the window and the loom[3], I would practise my writing and read the Bible.

3

The Christmas Market

Four years passed. We heard about the war with the French and we heard stories of battles on land and at sea. And on one summer evening in 1815, we heard of a great battle and a victory at Waterloo. But our lives did not change. However, in that same year, we heard news that changed our lives. The government put a new tax on corn.

'Bring me a mug of ale, Prue!' Gideon shouted when he came back from market with the news. 'It's the best news we've ever had. We'll plough up all our land and sow corn. The tax will make the corn dear. We'll sell our corn and we'll become rich!'

So now we were going to work harder than ever! Harder than we had worked for the past four years, from day-break until dark and after.

But I saw clearly that Gideon worked hard only to make money. He did not love the farm and the land as I did. Gideon wanted to make money to become rich – to leave the farm and go and live like a gentleman in Lullingford.

I grew taller and taller – and the hard work made me very slender[4]. Gideon also grew tall, and broad too. He was a very handsome young man.

The farm was doing very well now. We had a big flock of sheep and a herd of pigs that Mother looked after. After a time, we had enough money to buy two oxen, for ploughing.

'When we go to Lullingford to buy the oxen,' said Gideon, 'you can come too. You can look in the shop windows and I'll show you the house we are going to buy. But that won't be for a long time yet.'

I looked forward joyfully to the journey. I had not been to Lullingford since Father died. Lullingford had always seemed a wonderful place to me.

'But how will I go?' I asked.

I could not ride on our horse, behind Gideon, because of the big baskets that were full of goods for the market.

'Beguildy will let you do some leasing[3] in his fields,' said Gideon. 'You can sell the leasings and I'll use the money to hire[4] the miller's pony.'

'But what about Jancis?' I asked. 'Won't she want to do the leasing herself?'

17

'Don't be foolish. Jancis is too lazy to pick up one ear of corn. I like her because she is so beautiful. But she does not work hard.'

Since Father died, Gideon had thought of nothing but money. But now he often thought of Jancis too. They met on Sundays when Gideon didn't work.

Missis Beguildy told me how, every Sunday, Gideon came and knocked on their door. Jancis, dressed in her best gown, let him in. They sat down together on the settle[3]. And Mister Beguildy would look angrily at them. He did not want Jancis to marry a farmer. He had different plans for her.

But Missis Beguildy loved to see Gideon and Jancis together. Every Sunday, she tried to get Mister Beguildy to go out of the house. One day, she even set fire to the barn roof! Beguildy had to run to bring water to put the fire out.

In the end, Beguildy told Gideon to keep away. Then Gideon met Jancis in the woods, but Beguildy found out about that too. I believe that Gideon loved Jancis. But he was not going to marry until he became rich. Gideon told Jancis this and he was telling her the truth.

It was nearly Christmas before I could go to market. I was up at four in the morning. I tidied the house for Mother and got the things together ready to sell in the market.

Tivvy, Sexton's daughter, was coming to stay with Mother for the day. Tivvy came early because she was in love with Gideon. She was terribly jealous of Jancis and always called her the Wizard's daughter. But Gideon did not listen to her. He thought of no girl but Jancis.

The sun was rising as we set off for Lullingford. Gideon rode our horse, Bendigo. And I rode the miller's pony. I looked towards the blue hills. They looked wonderful to me. But Gideon kept looking behind him to Plash. I knew he was thinking of Jancis.

It was still early when we rode into Lullingford. Its broad street was quiet and peaceful. At one end of the street was the church with its tall steeple.

Then there were many shops selling many different things. And at the other end of the street was the smithy³. I remembered how pleasant it was to see the warm, friendly flames of the black-smith's fire.

Near the smithy, there was a row of little cottages. One of them belonged to the weaver³. But the old weaver had died and I wondered who lived there now. We had heard that the weaver's nephew had taken over his uncle's work.

The weaver's cottage faced south and there was a vine growing up all over the wall. I had been inside the cottage once, a long time ago. I remembered the big loom in the bright sitting-room and the little green lawn behind the house. To me, it seemed a house different from any other. But I did not know why.

The market was held in a square by the church. We put our baskets on the ground and were soon selling our goods. It was a happy day, full of noise and colour. And the church bells rang out every half-hour.

When we had sold everything, we went into the inn for something to eat. Some old men were sitting outside the inn. They were drinking mugs of ale and they were singing.

When Gideon and I went by, they stopped singing. They all stared in silence at me and my hare-lip.

'Don't drink when she's near,' said one old man. 'The ale will poison you.'

In the inn, I bent over my plate of food to hide my tears.

At that moment, a young lady – one of the gentry³ – came in. She was wearing a long, red riding-coat. She was a tall, handsome girl. Her eyes were as black as coal.

The lady looked around the room and saw me. Then she said with a laugh, 'We need a broomstick here, innkeeper.'

I knew she had been talking to the old men. Mother had told me once that talk about broomsticks was a way of saying that I was a witch.

The young lady was Miss Dorabella, the squire's daughter.

*The lady looked around the room and saw me. 'We need a
broomstick here, innkeeper.'*

She walked across the room to where her brother was standing.

'Who's the woman with the hare-lip?' she called out.

Her brother nodded towards Gideon and told Miss Dorabella to talk more quietly. When she saw Gideon, she called out, 'Why, it is young Sarn of Sarn!'

Gideon stood up and Miss Dorabella held out her hand.

'There's to be an election[4] soon,' she said. 'Father'll want you to work for him, Sarn. Or will you be too busy dancing on the mountainside with your Missis here? You'll look fine with your broomsticks and the moon shining!'

Gideon understood what she meant. His eyes went very dark – dark and cold with anger. He looked down at her and said, very clearly and slowly, 'Ma'am, this is my sister. If I want to dance with witches on the mountainside, I will. And if I want to dance at the hunt ball with the gentry, I'll do that too. But I won't ask you to be my partner.

'And maybe I won't vote for Squire at election time either. For how can a man govern the country, if he can't govern his own daughter? It's a pity he didn't beat you more often ma'am, when you were younger.'

Then Miss Dorabella's brother called to her and they both left the inn. Gideon sat down and went on eating his meal. But I was so unhappy that I could not eat anything.

Gideon went off to buy the oxen and I went to the shops. I bought a few presents for Christmas.

We packed everything away in the baskets and put them onto Bendigo's back. Then Gideon got onto the horse and I got onto the pony. Gideon took me along the road to the other side of town. I'd never been that way before because it wasn't on our way home.

We came to two big gates and went through them and along a drive[4]. At the end of the drive was another gate. Through this gate, I could see a big, grand house.

'This house is going to be ours one day,' said Gideon.

There were four windows on either side of the big door. There were eight windows above them and more windows in the roof. The house was dark and I thought it was a sad place although it was so big and grand.

'There is an old man living in the house now,' said Gideon. 'He'll die in about another ten years. By that time, we'll have enough money to buy the house.'

'Isn't the old man who lives here Miss Dorabella's uncle?' I said. 'Won't her brother, young Camperdine, want to live in the house?'

'No, he'll never want to live here. The house will be sold and we must work hard and have our money ready.'

We turned away from the closed gate and left the house. When we got back to the inn, everyone had gone home. We sat alone beside the warm, red fire.

After a while, Gideon began to speak very slowly.

'Now, Prue,' Gideon said, 'you must know how I feel about Jancis. And when Beguildy sent me away, I wanted to marry her more than ever.

'I wanted her so much that I almost decided to give up my plans. That's why I took you to see the big house.'

'Did you want to remind yourself of your plans?' I asked.

'Perhaps. I plan to get some learning from you, Prue. Then I'll become more powerful and people will respect me. Perhaps, I might one day marry Squire's daughter!'

'What! Miss Dorabella?'

'Why not? She's a woman, isn't she? She angers me and pleases me too. So I thought perhaps I'd give up Jancis. Another man can have her. She'll be happy enough when the babies come, whoever she marries.'

'Well, it seems you've made plans for everyone,' I said sadly.

I knew my brother was a strong man, but I did not think him so hard.

'But now I've decided,' Gideon went on. 'I won't give up Jancis and I won't give up the house either. I'll have both. Then I'll take Jancis to the hunt ball in a fine, silk gown. And if Miss Dorabella smiles at me, I'll have her too. I'll make Wizard's daughter my wife and Squire's daughter a whore[4]!'

And Gideon banged his hand down on the table.

'You are a hard man, even though you are my brother,' I told him.

'Maybe I am. But I can't change, Prue. It's how I was made. No one can change that.'

And then Gideon sat for a whole hour, without saying a word. I looked sadly at the fire and hoped that one day all would be well.

Finally, Gideon spoke, 'Aye[1], I'll marry Jancis and I'll buy the house or I'll die trying.'

And so now I knew we had all set out into a dark future – Gideon, Mother and me – and now Jancis too.

———

It was past midnight when we reached Sarn Mere. When we saw the light in the windows of our house, Gideon spoke, 'Well, I hope you enjoyed yourself today, Prue,' he said.

'Ah, it was a wonderful day and thank you kindly, Gideon lad.'

'And you agree to help?'

'Haven't I promised?' I said.

'But that was before Jancis,' Gideon answered.

'I agree to Jancis,' I said. 'And I'll work – I never was afraid of hard work.'

Mother and Tivvy were waiting for us. Mother was crying. She believed that we had been drowned in Sarn Mere.

'I'm staying the night here,' Tivvy said. 'It's too late now to go home. I'll sleep in your bed with you, Prue.'

Tivvy looked at Gideon and I could see how much she wanted him. But Gideon did not look at her. He had made his decision. He was going to marry Jancis.

But I didn't want to sleep with Tivvy. So I waited a while and then got the lantern and Father's old sheepskin coat. I went up into the attic, and wrapped myself up in the warm coat. Then I began to write in my book. I wrote down everything that had happened that day. I wanted to forget the unhappy things that had happened to me.

Because I had no lover, I wanted the world to love me. But when I showed myself to the world, the world laughed and turned away from me.

4

The Love-Spinning

Christmas came and went. We had no visitors at Sarn. Mother was ill and I had to stay at home to look after her.

But on New Year's Day, I went to Plash for a lesson again. I did the ploughing for Beguildy first. It was hard work driving the oxen over the frost-covered red earth.

I had just finished the ploughing when Jancis saw me. She and her mother came running out of the house, very excited. Jancis' face was rosy-red in the cold air. With her yellow hair, she looked as beautiful as a fairy.

'Prue, Prue!' Jancis called out. 'Gideon's promised to marry me! Yes, he's given his word. Oh, Prue, I'm so happy and excited!'

'Come inside, my dears,' Missis Beguildy said. 'I'll make some tea.'

So we sat together round the fire. Mister Beguildy wasn't pleased with the news. He looked very angry.

'Go and read your old books,' Missis Beguildy said. 'There's a lot to be done before the wedding.'

'Don't talk to me of weddings!' Beguildy shouted. 'I tell you, woman, I don't like this match[4]. Old Sarn hated me and his son hates me too. Anyway, my girl's too good to be a farmer's wife. Why

24

she's as beautiful as a flower! Any young lord would be happy to lie beside her!'

'Aye, lie beside her – but not to marry her!' Missis Beguildy shouted back.

'Who cares? He'd pay me, I'd see to that!' And Beguildy went into his room before anyone could answer him.

Jancis was crying at the thought of not marrying Gideon. But we told her she would marry Gideon. Then we sat drinking tea and making plans.

'We'll have a love-spinning[3], of course,' Missis Beguildy said. 'I'll invite everyone we know. You can write the letters, Prue. Then I'll ask the weaver to come. He can stay two or three days and weave the wedding sheets.

'And we'll have a caking too,' Missis Beguildy went on. 'The money we make from selling the cakes will pay the weaver.'

Jancis clapped her hands in excitement.

'Oh, a love-spinning!' she cried. 'What a time we'll have. And a caking too! Oh, how I love Gideon for asking me to marry him!'

Caking was an old custom, nearly forgotten now. It was a kind of gambling, playing for cakes instead of money. But how we women enjoyed it!

'Now, Prue,' Missis Beguildy went on, 'when you write the letters, you may say that Jancis Beguildy is to marry Gideon Sarn who lives on his own land at Sarn. And put down that the wedding will be as soon as possible.'

Beguildy put his head round the door of his room and shouted, 'Write down that you are all fools! Sarn Mere will dry up before this wedding takes place! Am I not the Wizard of Plash? Can't I see into the future?'

Beguildy became quieter when I told him how much I'd ploughed. He gave me my lesson as usual. I had no fear of the man, and before I left him, I said, 'Leave Jancis alone, Mister. She'll have enough trouble marrying a man like Gideon. If you try to stop the wedding, you may do harm.'

But Beguildy did not answer.

———

So Missis Beguildy invited her guests to the love-spinning. She baked a lot of cakes to sell to the women for a penny each. After a morning of spinning, we would all play cards for the cakes and a good player could win a basketful of them. We women led such dull lives that we enjoyed a caking more than anything else.

Mother had not been well that winter, but nothing would stop her from going to Jancis' love-spinning.

Mother and I were the first to arrive at Plash. Mister Beguildy was not at home so he would not spoil our day. Jancis ran out of the house and greeted us. Soon the other women arrived, and all together there were twelve of us. We started work at once. Our spinning-wheels made a pleasant humming sound. Then Jancis began singing and we all joined in.

Suddenly the door opened and the bright sun shone into the room where we were sitting.

A young man stood there, looking at us all. I had not seen him before. I knew that of all the men in the world he was the man I would love!

We were all silent. The young man took off his hat and said, 'Your servant, ladies. I'm the weaver.'

What did he look like? It is hard for me to say, for love looks with a different eye. But all the women stopped spinning and looked at him in silence.

I stayed in my corner where I could not be seen. I wanted this man to be my lover and my lord. But he would never want me for I was cursed with a hare-lip.

We all sat so silently that the young man laughed and said again, 'I'm the weaver, Kester Woodseaves.'

Then Missis Beguildy brought the young man to the fire and gave him food and drink. I stayed back where he could not see me.

'Oh, Mister Woodseaves, welcome,' said Jancis. 'I'm so glad

*I knew that of all the men in the world he was the man
I would love!*

you've come to weave for me. Will you come to my wedding if Prue writes you a letter?'

'Perhaps I will,' the weaver said with a smile. 'And who's Prue who is able to write letters?'

Before Jancis could answer, Felena, the shepherd's wife, leant forward.

'Sir,' she said, 'are you married?'

'Why, no, I'm not married,' the weaver answered quietly.

'And have you promised to marry anyone?'

'The answer's "no" to that too,' the weaver said. 'I live by myself and I'm a happy man.'

So the spinning began again and we spun even harder. A little later, Missis Beguildy took the weaver up to the attic, where the loom was.

When Missis Beguildy came down again, she said, 'Thank you all kindly for the spinning. We've spun enough yarn to keep that young man busy for two or three days. We'd better have the caking before Beguildy comes back.'

We sat down at the tables and Missis Beguildy brought out a big dish, piled high with cakes.

Felena, the shepherd's wife, sat next to me.

'I think we're too old to play for cakes, Prue Sarn,' she said. 'Let's pretend we're playing for the love of the weaver!'

'The weaver's love is none of our business,' I said. I found it difficult to speak when I thought of the young man upstairs.

'Why, Prue Sarn,' Felena said with a smile. 'Your face is burning red. What's the matter? Are you ill?'

I said nothing. I was angry, but I was pleased too. The beautiful Felena thought of me as a woman able to love and be loved.

'A man like the weaver is a man worth gambling for,' added Felena as we started to play.

Not a man worth gambling for, I whispered to myself. A man worth dying for!

I played cards and I won everything. No one could stop me.

When it was time to leave, Missis Beguildy thanked everyone. Then she turned to Mother.

'A lot's been spun,' she said, 'and I've sold enough cakes to pay the weaver. So you can tell your son, Missis Sarn, that we'll be ready with the bride and the linen when he tells us to prepare the marriage bed.'

When we got home, Gideon was waiting for us.

'It's been a wonderful day,' Mother told him. 'A day to remember. Prue won the game too. Look at the cakes we've got!'

This pleased Gideon, as he liked to do things well himself.

'And we met the young weaver,' Mother went on. 'Such a fine young man! One that any woman would like for a son.'

'Ah, that's Kester Woodseaves,' Gideon said. 'I've heard he's a fine wrestler[3]. He can read and write too.'

'Did you like the weaver, Prue?' Mother asked. 'You didn't speak to him, did you? Why did you hide yourself away?'

'Like him?' I said slowly. 'Oh, did I like him . . .?' And I stopped, afraid to show my feelings.

'Why, Prue, you're so tired that you're nearly asleep!' Gideon said. 'You'd better go to bed or you'll do no work tomorrow.'

But I was not tired, only happy and excited. I remembered the text in the Bible: 'The Master has come.' Yes, Kester Woodseaves was my master and I knew I'd have no other. The words were so sweet to me, that I wrote them in my book, in my best writing.

And so, at last, I fell asleep.

5

The Dark Road

The next morning, very early, Jancis came running down our path.

'What can I do?' she cried. 'What can I do? What will Sarn say? Oh, why was I born the Wizard's child?'

'Now sit down, Jancis,' I told her. 'I can't understand a word. Tell me exactly what's the matter.'

'Father met Squire's son, young Camperdine, yesterday,' Jancis said. 'Father told him that he could call up Venus[2], the goddess of love. Camperdine's promised to give Father five pounds if he does it!'

'But this is nonsense, Jancis,' I said. 'What has it to do with you?'

'Why, it's me who has to pretend to be Venus!' Jancis cried. 'Father wants to please the young squire. And it's going to happen the day after tomorrow, Prue!'

'But what does he want you to do?'

'I am to stand, all naked, with a light shining on me, like the goddess Venus herself. If Sarn ever found out that I had done this, he'd never speak to me again.'

'Then don't do it, Jancis.'

'But when I said no, Father beat me. And he says he'll beat me again. He wants that five pounds. What can I do?'

'How does Beguildy plan to do it?' I asked slowly. 'Won't the young squire know who you are?'

'Father said it'll be too dark to see my face,' Jancis said. 'There'll be a red light and some smoke. I'm to stand in the cellar, with a rope round me. Father will pull the rope and I'll come up through the trap-door[4] into his room. I'll stand there for a few moments and then go back down again.'

I thought again and then said slowly, 'Do you love Gideon?'

'Oh, yes, I do,' Jancis answered.

'When does the weaver leave?' I asked.

'The weaver?' Jancis asked in surprise. 'Why, he goes tomorrow.'

'Well then, Jancis, I'll do it for you,' I said.

'You!' And Jancis looked so surprised that I could have hit her.

'Yes, me – Prue Sarn. It's a funny thing for me to be a beautiful goddess. But no one will know. Your father will be in the kitchen. I'll put a piece of cloth over my head, to cover my face and dark hair. The young squire will see what he's come to see – a naked woman. He'll pay the money and your father will be happy.'

'Oh, Prue, you are good! I do love you so,' Jancis cried. 'And it won't matter to you at all because you'll never have a lover.'

'Go away now,' I said, suddenly angry. 'We'll talk about it tomorrow. Now go – quickly!'

———

The time for Camperdine to see Venus came. I felt afraid and ashamed.

But when I was standing there, being pulled up in a cloud of smoke, I did not know whether to laugh or cry. For here was Prue Sarn, the girl with the Devil's mark, playing the part of the goddess of love and beauty!

As I stood there in the red light, with the cloth over my head, I saw the young squire lean forward towards me, his arms outstretched.

I heard a sound from the other side of the room and turned my head. Then I nearly cried out, for there sat Kester Woodseaves!

How unlucky I was! Here was the one man in the world I loved, but the one man I wanted to hide from.

The weaver was leaning forward too. Yes, although I had the Devil's curse, two men found me beautiful that night.

And how could I be ashamed when my master had seen me and desired me?

*For here was Prue Sarn, the girl with the Devil's mark, playing
the part of the goddess of love and beauty!*

I was only in the room for a minute. Down in the cellar again, I heard Beguildy say, 'Well, gentlemen, have I earned my five pounds?' And young Camperdine answered, 'Indeed you have – and more.'

So I got dressed and ran home. I did not speak to Jancis.

From that night on, I was the bride of the weaver. Whatever I did in the fields or in the house, I thought of Kester Woodseaves and remembered his smile.

It was still winter and Sarn Mere was covered with ice. But in my heart, spring had come. I wrote in my book: *The first day of spring.* For my master had looked at me and found me beautiful.

———

All through the cold days, Gideon and I were hard at work. We ploughed and ploughed for Gideon would grow nothing but corn.

'The new laws will keep the price of corn high,' Gideon told me. 'When this corn is grown, we'll be rich, Prue. And when we've got the money, we'll leave this old place and never think of it again.'

'I can't understand you, Gideon,' I said. 'You work so hard, but you don't love the land at all.'

'No, and I don't love money either.'

'Then what do you want, Gideon?' I asked.

'I want to be the best. To win all and take all. That's how I was made and I can't change. Why do you bother about it, Prue? We're working for the future, aren't we?'

'But the future's something we can't plan for,' I said.

'The future's as you make it,' Gideon replied. 'I know my future and I'm ready to work for it.'

Later on, I told Mother what Gideon had said.

'I can't work hard much longer,' Mother said sadly. 'You must tell him, Prue, that I can't look after the pigs any longer. They go down by the water and my feet get so wet and cold.'

I had seen that Mother looked tired and ill all that winter. Next morning, I spoke to Gideon about it.

'Gideon,' I said. 'Mother's not well. She wants to rest. You must get a lad to look after the pigs.'

'Must? Who says must to me?' Gideon shouted. 'I'm master of Sarn, aren't I?'

'But you must not drive Mother to death,' I told him. 'Get a lad for the pigs, Gideon.'

Gideon stared at me angrily.

'If you want a lad, why don't you get married? You can get a lad that way! That is, if you can find anyone who will marry you!'

I turned away. It was a long time before I forgot my brother's cruel words.

Now at last, spring had come. A warm wind began to blow. Flowers were growing. Sometimes I sang as I ploughed. Even Mother became a little happier.

One afternoon in late spring, when we were having our tea by the window, Mother suddenly said, 'We'll have the weaver.'

I gave a gasp, but said nothing.

'Yes, we'll have the weaver, Mister Woodseaves,' Mother repeated. 'I like the best weaving.'

I fell into a dream. If Kester came to weave for us, he'd work in our attic. He'd walk about there and look out of the window. And ever after, when I sat there, Kester would be in the attic with me. Just as he always was in my heart.

Mother put on her spectacles and looked at me. She gave a little smile.

'Yes, we'll have the weaver,' she said quietly.

———

The next day, Jancis came into the dairy where I was making butter.

'Oh, Prue!' she cried. 'The young squire's been talking to Father again. He thinks I was Venus and Father does too, of course. Now the young man wants me for himself. If I don't agree, Father says he'll send me away to work as a dairymaid[3] somewhere. I'll be away for three years. Can't Gideon marry me now?'

I shook my head.

'He won't do that,' I said. 'You'll have babies. Gideon would have to spend money on them, wouldn't he?'

'Oh, dear! What can I do?' Jancis cried.

At that moment, Gideon came into the dairy. He stood there, strong and handsome. I understood why Jancis wanted to marry him.

Gideon looked at Jancis. Her yellow hair was the colour of cream. She looked like a rose in her pink gown.

'You're early. Why are you here?' Gideon asked.

'I've got news,' Jancis said quickly. Then she stopped and looked at me.

'Beguildy wants to sell the child, Gideon,' I said. 'To sell her to the squire's son, for his pleasure.'

'What! Sell my girl? I'll kill the man!'

'She's not sold yet,' I said. 'But if Jancis doesn't agree, Beguildy'll send her to the Hiring Fair[3]. She'll be hired out for three years. She'll have to go and live on a farm far beyond Lullingford.'

'I don't want to go away!' Jancis cried. 'I'm your true love Gideon, indeed I am.'

I waited for Gideon to speak, but he said nothing.

'Please don't let Jancis be sent away, Gideon,' I said.

Jancis took his hand and kissed it.

'Oh, be my sweetheart, Sarn,' she said.

Gideon groaned.

'You're dragging me down to poverty,' he said. 'If I marry you now, I'll never get on. I'll have no money for years and years. And if I take Jancis away from Camperdine, he'll become my enemy. What's made the man so mad for Jancis?'

Jancis looked at me. But I could not tell Gideon the truth.

'It would only delay your plans for a little while, Gideon,' I said softly. 'You'll have the money later.'

'No,' he said. His face became hard. 'We won't marry now. We must wait three years. But I don't want to,' he added quietly.

The three of us stood there. Then Gideon took a step towards

Jancis. If he takes her in his arms, I thought, all will be well. But he said, 'Three years isn't a long time. By then, all our land will be growing corn and we'll be reaping what we have sown.'

'I pray we don't reap sadness and curses,' I said. 'The corn will bring us gold, but I fear the gold. Perhaps gold is the "precious bane" I've read about. It's valuable, but at the same time it's a curse to all. Perhaps it will destroy us all.'

'I don't care what name you give it, as long as it brings me the things I want,' said Gideon. 'And don't think I'm afraid of Beguildy! I'll tell him so on Sunday.'

'Oh, why can't people be happy together?' Jancis cried out. 'Why must you be so cruel, Sarn?'

She walked sadly to the door.

'Listen, the wind's getting stronger,' she said. 'It's bringing us bad luck, I'm sure.'

Gideon took her and kissed her, but it did not make him change his mind.

At last, Jancis turned away and said, 'I must go. The sun's gone down and there's darkness before me. I see a dark road, going down into the water. Don't let me walk down that road, Sarn!'

And in a moment she had gone, walking alone through the wind and the dark woods.

6

The Hiring Fair

It was May Day, the day of the Hiring Fair. We had a lot of goods for market. So I hired the miller's pony again and set off with Gideon very early.

The air was full of the smell of flowers. There was no wind, and in the morning light everything looked clear and fresh.

'I wonder where poor Jancis will sleep tonight,' I said sadly.

'At Grimble's farm,' Gideon answered.

'How do you know, before the hiring, Gideon?'

'I know Missis Grimble wants a dairymaid,' Gideon answered. 'It's far away and young Camperdine will not find her there.'

'She'll be terribly lonely,' I said.

'You can write me a letter for her, Prue,' said Gideon.

'I'll do it gladly, lad,' I said. 'But how will she answer?' For Jancis, like Gideon, could not read or write.

Gideon smiled.

'Oh, I've thought of that,' he said. 'Grimble's farm is such a big place they have the weaver there every month or two. Weaver can write for Jancis.'

'Do you mean Mister Woodseaves?' I said and Gideon nodded.

So here was a strange thing indeed! I was to write love letters for my brother. And the man I loved would read them and send back answers for me to read.

Then I knew what I would do. I would write all that was in my heart – things that Gideon would never say or think of. And Kester Woodseaves would read my words and answer them with his own!

It was all so strange and twisted that I began to laugh aloud.

When we reached Lullingford, the Hiring Fair was just beginning. Beguildy was already there with Jancis. She was holding her milking-stool[3] and very pretty she looked too.

Jancis was talking to Grimble and his Missis.

'The Grimbles don't look kind folk,' I said. 'Why must she go there, Gideon?'

'It's a big place. They'll give more money. We must think of that first.'

Gold, always gold, I thought. Gold, that precious bane that might destroy us all.

Gideon went up and spoke to the Grimbles, to decide the wages. Jancis called across to Beguildy and said, 'Missis Grimble will hire me, Father.'

'Oh, will she?' Beguildy said, coming over. 'And what will you give me for three years?' he asked Missis Grimble.

'Eighteen pounds.'

'Make it twenty and you can have her. She's strong. You can make her work hard. You can give her a beating if she needs it.'

'If anyone touches my girl, it'll be the worse for you, Beguildy!' Gideon shouted. 'And Jancis is to have the money, not you!'

'And who are you, to say that?' Beguildy shouted back. 'Gideon Sarn, Sin Eater and a man cursed!'

In answer, Gideon hit Beguildy so hard that he fell down.

'I'll get you for that blow, Sarn!' the old man shouted. 'I curse you! I curse you in house and meadow. By fire and water I curse you! Nothing you do will succeed from this time on!'

Gideon turned away and did not listen to Beguildy.

Gideon took Jancis to see the big house that he had shown me. The house where Jancis would one day live like a lady.

I stayed behind in the market. Our goods sold quickly. There were a lot of people in Lullingford that day who had come for the bull-baiting[3].

Soon people began to leave the market-place. I sat there waiting for Gideon to return.

Missis Grimble came across and spoke to me.

'You're the sister of my new dairymaid's young man, aren't you?' she said. 'Are they going to get married?'

'Oh, yes,' I said.

'That's good,' Missis Grimble said. 'I like my maids to have a young man – as long as he's far away.' Then looking at my hare-lip, she added, 'It's a sad thing for a young woman to be so cursed.'

The day seemed to go dark. Tears came into my eyes and I turned my head away.

A young man was walking along the quiet street. It was the weaver – Kester Woodseaves!

He was wearing his best clothes – a green coat, a flowered waistcoat and a black hat.

'Weaver, Weaver!' Missis Grimble called. 'When are you coming to work for me again?'

He walked over towards us. I stood up so quickly that I knocked over a pot of flowers. I ran behind a waggon. The weaver must not see my face!

'What's the matter with the girl?' Missis Grimble shouted out. 'Most girls stay when a young man comes near, but she runs away!'

'Who is she?' asked Kester. I could hear his voice clearly.

'Why, she's Prue Sarn, young Sarn's sister. She's got a hare-lip. Maybe that makes her strange. Some say she's a witch . . .'

Kester said nothing, but began to put the flowers back in the pot. Then he said clearly so that I could hear, 'She's got a very slender, beautiful figure.' And I thanked him in my heart for his kind words.

'Are you going to the bull-baiting, Mister Woodseaves?' Missis Grimble asked.

'Why, the answer to that is yes and no,' the weaver said with a smile.

'What do you mean?'

'You'll see in a short time. Good-day, Missis.'

And the weaver went on up the street.

I waited for a while and then came out from behind the waggon. I began to follow Kester Woodseaves.

He walked to the green meadow outside the town where the bull-baiting was to be held. And I walked after him, hiding my face with my bonnet[4].

There was a great crowd in the meadow. I thought what a sad thing it was that people had come to see a bull being baited by a dog.

Mister Callard's white bull stood in the middle of the meadow. It was chained to a post. All around, people were shouting, children were screaming and dogs were barking. I saw Kester in the crowd and moved closer to him.

I wondered what a man like Kester was doing at a baiting. Somehow, I knew he was there to do good. And I knew that I had to stay near him. I had a strange feeling that he would need my help that day.

7

The Baiting

Some men were standing together, each man with one or two dogs. The men looked cruel and ugly. Their dogs were fierce and ugly too, with great, sharp teeth.

The men all turned towards Kester as he walked up to them.

Farmer Huglet, a tall, fat man, looked at Kester.

'Where's your dog, Mister?' he asked. Huglet was holding two very fierce dogs.

'Why, that's the weaver,' Mister Grimble said. 'Where's your dog, Weaver?'

'I've no dog.'

'No dog? Then stand back, so we can start the baiting!'

But Kester did not move. He stood there, slim and straight. Kester looked at the crowd calmly and then back at the men with dogs.

'I want you men to stop this,' he said.

There was a long silence. Then Huglet shouted with laughter and Grimble smiled too.

'Stop it?' Huglet roared. 'Stop the bull-baiting? You can't stop it!'

'I want to stop baiting all over England,' the weaver answered quietly.

'And why do you want that?' Grimble asked in a quiet voice.

'Because it's cruel.'

'It isn't cruel. The dogs like it. And the bull does too!' Huglet shouted.

'Who cares if they like it?' Grimble said. 'I like it. And that's enough for me!'

'What do you want to stop the baiting for?' Mister Callard called out.

'I've said why,' the weaver replied. 'Now look, Mister Callard, the bull's yours. Will you sell it to me? I'll give you a good price.'

'I can't do that,' Mister Callard answered. 'Why, if the bull wins, I'll get twenty pounds!'

'Then I'll give you twenty pounds and you can take the bull home with you.'

Callard stared at Kester, too surprised to speak. But his wife pushed forward and said, 'Take the money, my dear. Take the twenty pounds and we'll take the bull home again!'

'Take it home! Never. You can't spoil our sport³ for twenty pounds!' Huglet shouted.

Kester said nothing. He took out a bag of coins and offered the money to Callard.

Callard held out his hand, but Huglet pushed him back.

'We want our sport, I tell you!' he shouted. And all the men with dogs repeated his words.

'That's right. We want our sport!'

'What a pity it is,' Kester said, 'to make one animal fight another. If you want sport, why don't you wrestle? Come on, I'll wrestle with each of you, one by one.'

Nobody said anything. They all knew what a good wrestler Kester was.

Mister Grimble looked at Kester with hate in his eyes. He smiled and then looked round at the people.

'I'll agree with you if you'll do one thing,' he said.

'What's that?' Kester said.

'Fight with the dogs yourself!'

Grimble laughed and Huglet laughed even louder.

'You'd like to see a man baited like a bull, wouldn't you, Mister Grimble?' said Kester quietly. 'All right, I'll fight each dog, one by one. I won't kill them, but I'll chain them up.

'And if I do it,' Kester went on, 'I want your promise that there won't be a bull-baiting in Lullingford for another ten years. But if I fail to put a chain on any dog, then the baiting goes on.'

41

Everyone began talking and shouting. At first, Mister Huglet could not speak, he was laughing too much. Then he shouted, 'If you agree lads, put up your hands!'

All hands went up.

'Right!' Huglet cried. 'That's agreed.'

Now my love for Kester made me feel strong. I was ready to do anything to help him. I went quietly to a shop and stole a long knife. I hid it under my skirt. It was there if I needed it.

All the men stood round in a circle. Kester stood in the middle with the chains. The fierce dogs were barking loudly. They were wild dogs, trained to fight.

The first dog was set free.

'At him! Bite him!' shouted his master.

Then something strange happened – so strange that I could not believe it. Kester stepped forward. Very quietly, he said, 'Good dog, Bingo. Come on. We're friends, aren't we?'

Immediately, the dog started to wag its tail and lick Kester's hand. He quietly put a chain round the dog's neck.

Huglet looked very angry, but he could say nothing.

It was the same with the next dog and the next. Kester chained them all and gave them to their masters.

'I like dogs,' he said. 'All these dogs here are my friends.'

'Right,' said Grimble. 'But you don't know my dog, Toby. And you won't make friends with him.'

Grimble spoke the truth. Toby did not know Kester and did not want to make friends with him. But Kester got the chain round the dog's neck. Then, suddenly, the dog jumped up at Kester and bit him deep in the throat.

I caught hold of Grimble. 'Take your dog off!' I shouted. But Grimble didn't move. One second more and my beloved would be dead. I rushed forward.

As the great dog stood with its teeth in my master's throat, I pushed the knife deep into the beast's heart. Blood poured out. The dog fell dead and Kester fell down in a faint[4] beside it.

42

Then, suddenly, the dog jumped up at Kester and bit him deep in the throat.

'Water!' I cried. 'Bring water!'

An apothecary[3] from Lullingford was in the crowd. He bent over Kester and looked at his throat.

'I must burn this bite with hot iron,' the apothecary said. 'But we need a fire to heat the iron.'

I stood up, afraid of no one.

'Quick!' I shouted. 'Get sticks, light a fire, you men. Do it or you are all murderers!'

People moved quickly as though they were afraid of me. Soon a fire was blazing. I put the iron knife in the fire to make it hot. The apothecary poured brandy down Kester's throat. Then the man placed the burning hot iron of the knife on the bite.

Kester gave a terrible cry.

'There, there, my dear,' I whispered. 'It's done. You are safe now.'

'We were just in time,' the apothecary said.

'We had to be in time,' I said, 'for I am his guardian angel[2] for this day.'

Then everything began to turn round and round. I fell back on the ground in a faint. When I woke up, only Gideon and Jancis were there. All the other people had gone.

'Where is he?' I asked.

'Who?' said Jancis. 'The weaver? They've taken him back to Lullingford. He'll be well looked after.'

'You saved that man's life,' Gideon told me. 'I could not believe it when you took out that knife and killed Grimble's dog.'

'Prue is too shocked to ride home,' Jancis said softly to Gideon. 'Shall I ask the miller to take her home in his cart, Sarn? Perhaps I can go back with you to help Prue with the work – just for a day or two?'

'Ask Miller to take Prue, Jancis. But you can't come back. You know you've got to work at Grimble's.'

'Oh, I don't want to go there,' Jancis said, beginning to cry. 'Don't make me do it, Sarn.'

'I've showed you the place where you'll live like a lady one day, haven't I?' Gideon said. 'But first you must work three years at Grimble's. I have made my decision. Tears won't change it.'

So Jancis went to Grimble's and I went home slowly in the miller's cart. Gideon rode ahead on Bendigo.

When we got home, I told Mother the story.

'Why, Prue, you might have been killed!' she cried out.

She made some food and we sat down to eat. Mother sat down with us, asking Gideon question after question.

At last, Mother nodded her head several times and said, 'When summer comes, I'll have the weaver. There'll be enough yarn then to have the weaver.'

8

Letters

At the end of June, Mother said that she was going to have the weaver.

'I've spun such a lot of yarn that I must have the weaver. I'll send for him now.'

But I did not want Kester to see my face. The day he was coming, I said to Mother, 'I'll be working in the far meadow all day. I'll take bread and cheese so that I don't have to come back for food.'

'Oh you silly, silly girl,' Mother whispered. But she could not make me stay.

When I got home in the evening, the weaver had gone. But there were bits of wool on the attic floor and a pleasant smell of tobacco from his pipe.

Mother was full of praise for Kester Woodseaves – such a kind young man. He'd been like a son to her.

'Weaver wanted to know if I had any children besides Sarn,' Mother went on. 'So I told him.'

'Oh, Mother, what did you say?' I cried.

'I told him I had a daughter, the best girl in the world. And I told him that she was very tall and slender. And that she had long, silky hair and lovely dark eyes. And I told him how she was a scholar too, for she could both read and write.'

'What a story you made out of nothing, Mother,' I said.

'No story, my dear, because it's all true,' she answered.

'Did you tell Weaver I had a hare-lip?'

'No, my dear!' Mother cried. 'Why should I do that?'

'Well, he may think of me now and then, and if he ever saw me . . .'

'If he ever saw you, he'd like you very well,' Mother said with a smile. And then she added, 'Prue, would you care if the weaver had only one arm or only one leg?'

'Care, Mother?' I cried out without thinking. 'Why, I'd love him all the more for it!'

Mother smiled.

'I knew you loved the man, Prue. I just knew it. And I'm very glad that you do. But don't hide from him, Prue. Don't hide.'

'It was unkind of you to trick me like that,' I said. 'I didn't want to tell anyone about my love for the weaver.'

'I wanted to be sure, Prue,' Mother answered. 'And I do believe that all will be well with you one day. The weaver told me that he wasn't married. But if he did marry it would be to a girl like you.'

———

At the end of the corn harvest, Gideon asked me to write a letter to Jancis.

'What will I say in the letter?' I asked.

'Tell her about the farm and about the corn harvest,' said Gideon. 'And tell her about . . . Oh, you know what to write, Prue. I leave it to you.'

46

And so I was able to write what I pleased. And I knew who was going to read it – Weaver. So I wrote a letter from my heart to my beloved. And this is what I wrote:

Sarn
September Twenty-six

My dear sweetheart,
    The corn is now harvested and it is winter once again. Perhaps I'll see you at the Christmas market.
    I can see you and Weaver sitting together – you telling him what to say and he writing it all down and smiling sweetly.
    Tell Weaver that Huglet's got a terrible fierce dog now and to take care if he goes anywhere near.
    If Weaver wants any sewing done, my mother or sister will gladly do it for him.
    The harvest's not so good. Tell Mister Grimble I'd like a few lambs – good ones though, or I'll send them back.
    Goodbye and take care of yourself. A good cure for a cold is a hot drink of lemon and honey. You are my dearest, dearest love and I'd willingly die for you at any time – by the bite of dog or any other way, my dear.
    And so goodnight, from your lover,

Gideon Sarn

It was nearly Christmas when the answer came back from Jancis.

The High Farm, Outrack
December First

My dearest sweetheart,
    I write this to the best of lovers.
    Mister Woodseaves would be grateful for the sewing. Kind of you to remember it, Sarn. Perhaps you'd tell your sister.
    Mister Woodseaves says the cure for the cold is the best ever, but it needs a woman to make it properly.

Do not worry about Huglet's dog – Weaver's not afraid. But that was a brave woman who saved Weaver at the baiting. Mister Woodseaves heard that it was a tall, slim woman with beautiful dark eyes. Weaver says that if ever he had a sweetheart, he'd like one who looked like that.

And so goodnight and a merry Christmas from,

Jancis Beguildy

And so time went on for another year, and at last it was Christmas Eve again. It was a year and eight months since Kester had stopped the baiting.

There had been no letters from Jancis for a long time. But Gideon wasn't worried. The roads were so bad around Grimble's farm that no one could get to it in bad weather. So I thought sadly of Jancis, cut off from us by snow and high mountains.

That Christmas Eve, the house was very quiet. Mother was in bed. In bad weather, she often stayed in bed. Gideon was cutting wood. I could hear the sound of the axe.

I was baking, so the kitchen was warm and full of the smell of good bread. I'd made lots of pies for Christmas. The animals were all shut up for the night and the cat was sleeping peacefully by the fire.

I was singing quietly to myself, when I heard a quiet knock at the door. Who could it be? I opened the door.

And there, white and pale in the light of the fire, was Jancis. I pulled her inside and the poor girl fell down in a faint on the floor.

Her clothes were torn and wet. Her face and hands were covered in cuts and scratches.

When she woke up, Jancis told me she'd had no food for two days. She'd run away from Grimble's and had walked all the way back to Sarn.

'Oh, Prue, don't be angry!' Jancis cried. 'I could not stay there any longer. No one could stay there. And Christmas came and there was no news from Sarn. That made everything worse.'

'What are you going to say to Gideon, Jancis?' I asked.

'I don't care what he says, Prue, but please don't send me away tonight.'

I knew I was not going to do that. I made her comfortable on the settle by the fire. Jancis was so tired that she fell asleep at once.

When Gideon came in and saw her lying there he became terribly angry.

'Why, she'll lose all the money!' he cried. 'She won't even be paid for the time she's worked. That's three years' wages she's lost by running away!'

'How can you think of money when Jancis lies half-dead?' I shouted. 'You should thank me for saving your sweetheart from death, this day!'

Gideon looked surprised, but said nothing. He looked down at Jancis, who was awake now.

'So you've broken your time and come back,' he said angrily.

Jancis began to cry.

'No, don't do that,' Gideon said. 'Prue will shout at me again if you cry. I can see that Grimble hasn't fed you well. Did young Camperdine come looking for you?'

'No, Sarn,' Jancis whispered.

'Has any other young man been after you?' Gideon asked.

'No, Sarn. But Grimble's son wanted me. That's why I ran away. You're the only man I want, Sarn.'

'So you came back all those miles just for me, Jancis?'

'It's true, Sarn, I did.'

'Then give me a kiss, my girl!'

I ran out into the dairy to leave them alone. The cat ran after me, for she was always a little afraid of Gideon.

How I wished I was sitting on the settle with a young man's arm around me! And I knew the man I would choose.

'I can't have what I want, Pussy,' I said to the cat. 'But you can. What you want, you can have.'

And I gave the cat a bowl of cream.

I went back into the house to make Mother's tea. When I told

49

her about Jancis, Mother said, 'But why didn't the girl go home to Plash?'

'She's afraid of Beguildy, I suppose,' I said. 'I'll go and tell Missis Beguildy later. But let Jancis have her Christmas here.'

'You can stay here for Christmas,' I told Jancis. 'I'll go and see your mother on Boxing Day[4]. She can tell your father you're back. And after that, who knows? Maybe Gideon . . .'

Gideon heard what I was saying to Jancis.

'If you mean "maybe Gideon will marry you",'he said, 'I'll do that when I want to and not before. But I've told Jancis, if the harvest is good, we'll be married soon after. She's willing as well.'

'I'm glad,' I said. 'If you love anyone, you want them with you all the time, not far away.'

And that reminded me of a little house, not very far away, where the weaver lived.

'Jancis,' I said, 'you should send a letter to Mister Woodseaves. To let him know where you are.'

'All right, Prue,' she said. 'You can write. It's you that does the writing.'

Sarn
Christmas Eve

Dear Mister Woodseaves,

 I write to tell you I've left Missis Grimble. She's a hard woman and I was always hungry. I'm now at Sarn. Gideon and me hope to marry after harvest. Indeed, I'm glad of it, for when you love someone, you want to be with them all the time. If they're away, you cannot rest for worry, thinking that they may be lonely.

 I love my master more than anyone else in the world. He is so brave and good – he will always be my master. I love him more than I can say and will do so till the end of time.

 So goodnight, Mister Woodseaves, and a merry Christmas.

   From,
   Jancis Beguildy

Then I fastened the letter up and left it for Gideon to take to Lullingford next market-day.

———

That was the best Christmas we ever had at Sarn, with more laughing and singing than I could ever remember. Mother got up on Christmas Day and sat by the fire. As she looked at Jancis, I could see she was thinking of the grandchildren to come.

'Marry after the harvest, Sarn,' Mother said. 'Don't wait any longer. I may not live another winter and I do want to see you and Jancis married.'

'We won't wait long,' Gideon said, 'for I'll be a rich man when we've sold the corn. And in another two or three years, we'll be ready to move into the big house.'

On Boxing Day, I walked over to the Beguildys' house at Plash. Beguildy was away and I was able to have a long talk with Missis Beguildy.

'Callard needs a girl,' Missis Beguildy told me. 'Maybe they'll take Jancis there.'

So I said I'd ask the Callards myself and I went there the next day. The snow was very deep and it was bitterly cold. But I sang as I walked. Then I saw Callard's bull in a field. It was the same white bull that Kester had saved from the dogs. And thinking of Kester made me very happy.

The Callards were kind people and they agreed to take Jancis for six months and pay her good wages. So the next day, I drove Jancis over to Callard's farm in the waggon. I stopped at Plash on the way, to tell Beguildy what had happened.

I had never seen Beguildy so angry. And, to make it worse, he blamed everything on Gideon. But Missis Beguildy was pleased at the thought of the wedding in the autumn, after the harvest.

'The autumn roses will be out then, Jancis, and you shall carry some,' she said.

'And I say Sarn won't have my daughter!' Beguildy shouted.

'I've cursed the man by fire and water and cursed he will be! He and Jancis will never be married, believe me.'

There was no arguing with the man, so I said politely, 'Well, good-day to you, Mister Beguildy,' for I thought it was time to go on.

Between Plash and Callard's farm, Jancis looked at me with her big, blue eyes and said, 'Prue, why did you kill Grimble's dog and save Weaver's life? It was a very strange thing to do for someone you didn't know. Everyone says so.'

I did not answer, but I felt my face go red as fire.

'I wonder what Weaver would think if he knew!' Jancis went on.

'Well, he didn't know. He'd fainted,' I answered quickly.

'But maybe someone will tell him. What do I say if Weaver asks me?'

'Say nothing.'

'But the way you stood over him, like his guardian angel, with that great knife in your hand!'

'It's none of your business what I did.'

'Oh, yes it is. Because I love you, Prue,' Jancis said softly.

I said nothing and was thankful when we reached the Callards' gate.

Just before I drove away, Jancis called out, 'I shall have to send for Weaver soon.'

'What for?' I asked.

'To write me a letter for Sarn.'

'Why, you'll only be two or three miles away. What do you want to write a letter for?'

Jancis laughed.

'Why, that's none of your business, Prue Sarn,' she said. 'And that's what you said to me, didn't you?'

9

Down by the Mere

So Jancis was at Callard's and Gideon visited her every Sunday. During the week, he worked as hard as three men. I worked hard too and our farm had never looked so well. Every field was rich with golden corn. To Gideon, the corn *was* gold. I sometimes saw him looking at it, as a miser[4] looks at his money.

The best time of year at Sarn Mere was early summer. All round the Mere there were trees with beautiful green leaves. And the birds sang in the trees all day long. And the white and gold flowers of the water-lilies shone in the water.

There was one day in that early summer that I remember so clearly. I had forgotten my work on the farm and was watching the dragon-flies[4] dancing over the still water of the Mere.

Then I remembered that I had work to do. So I turned from the water and the dragon-flies. But just as I turned, I heard a noise and there stood Kester Woodseaves!

I thought of running away or even jumping in the Mere, but he put his hand on my shoulder. It was a strong, wrestler's hand and I could not move.

'Why do you want to run away, Prue Sarn?' Kester said gently. 'Why?'

I lowered my head, so that he could not see my face. But I said nothing.

'I do think it's unfair of you to run away from a man who has come specially to see you, Prue. Especially a man who has come to thank you for saving his life.

'What were you looking at when I came?' he added.

'Dragon-flies,' I replied.

'Yes, they are beautiful to watch and they fly so high,' said Kester.

53

'Yes. They fly so high that I sometimes think they reach up to heaven,' I said.

'We'd all like to do that,' Kester answered, 'but I'd like to have my heaven here on earth before I die.'

I was so interested in what Kester said that I forgot my hare-lip. I looked up at him and asked quietly, 'And what would your heaven be?'

'I'm not quite sure yet,' Kester answered. 'But in about a year's time, I think I'll know.'

'A year?' I said, smiling. 'That's a long time to spend choosing your little bit of heaven, isn't it?'

'Could you choose your heaven more quickly, Prue Sarn?' Kester asked me gently.

I looked at Kester's green coat and at the place, near his heart, where I wanted to put my head.

'Ah, I know what my heaven would be,' I said.

'Oh, then what is it?'

'Well, Mister Woodseaves, I think my thoughts are my own,' I answered with a smile.

He laughed.

'Well, you can write a good letter, Prue.'

'Those were Gideon's letters,' I said quickly.

'Then it was very kind of Gideon to tell me about a cure for a cold and offer to help with my sewing. It's not often a man thinks of such things.'

Kester looked at me with his clear, blue eyes and I lowered my head again.

'And Jancis writes nice letters too,' Kester said. 'I liked her letters. She sounds a nice girl. I remember that she wrote: "I love my master more than anyone else in the world . . . I love him more than I can say and will do so till the end of time."

'And there was another bit too,' Kester went on, '". . . and die for you . . . by the bite of dog or any other way, my dear."

'Wait a minute though,' Kester added. 'It was Sarn who said

54

'I'd like to have my heaven here on earth before I die.'

that to Jancis Beguildy. What a lover the man must be! Well, I'll be coming to help with the harvest. So I'll be sure to thank Sarn for all his good advice.'

'Oh, don't do that!' I cried.

'Why, what a strange girl, not wanting her brother to be thanked!'

But there was a pleased look on Kester's face. He'd found out what he wanted to know.

'Well, it's no use saying more,' Kester said with a smile. 'You wrote the letters and you made them up. And the man you were thinking of when you wrote them is a lucky man.'

'I haven't got a sweetheart,' I said.

'Well, I think that's a pity,' Kester answered. 'But anyway you've got a friend. When you go back to the house you can write in your book that Kester Woodseaves is your friend till time stops.'

Then we talked about the dragon-flies and other things and a very pleasant time we had together. It was a long time before I remembered to ask Kester how he knew about my book.

'There's not much I don't know about you, Prue,' Kester said.

Oh, how sweet were those words of his! Then I saw the evening shadows on the water. I remembered all the work that was still to be done. I turned to go.

'There's one thing I must ask you before you go,' said Kester.

And Kester looked down into my eyes, for he was just a little taller than me.

'Why did you do what you did at the baiting?' he asked. 'Getting the knife and killing that dog to save me?'

There was silence. What could I say?

'Why, I was your guardian angel for that day,' I said.

'Then if I ever need the help of an angel again, I will ask you,' Kester said.

And I could hear him laughing as he walked away through the wood.

10

The Harvest

Harvest time came at last. Never in my life had I seen a harvest like it. In field after field, the corn shone like gold.

Gideon and I started reaping at the beginning of August. How hard we worked to cut the corn! And the weather was fine, so we left the corn sheaves[3] there in the fields.

And so, at last, Gideon's dream was coming true. For the price of corn was high – so high that when Gideon sold it he would be a rich man.

I was happy too. Kester was coming to help with the harvest. Then he was going to London to learn to weave[3] with colours. When he came back home again, my hare-lip would be cured. I would be beautiful as a fairy for the man I loved.

We had a custom then called the love-carriage. After the corn had been cut, every family would bring its waggon to the fields. The corn sheaves would be put onto the waggons. Then the sheaves would be taken to the farmer's yard, to be piled up into great square ricks[3].

Our love-carriage was on a perfect day in mid-September. The sky was a deep, clear blue, with not a cloud to be seen. The waggons came early and every man worked as though the corn was his own.

About noon, when everyone was resting, I walked up to a high field to look for Kester. I saw him coming across the far meadows. When he saw me, he waved his hat and smiled.

Although he came late, Kester worked as hard as any other man. Now and again, I saw him looking at me with his laughing eyes. Once, he came over to me and said quietly, 'You still move away from me, Prue Sarn. You must come nearer, not move away.'

I went on picking up corn and did not answer.

So with a laugh in his voice, Kester said, 'There, there my dear! You are safe now!'

Kester looked straight into my eyes as he spoke. I felt my face becoming red. I knew now that Kester had heard my words at the baiting. And with a sweet smile, Kester went back to his work.

Ah, what a day that was! We worked and worked. Every armful of corn was like pure gold. Before sunset, they were loading the last waggon and all the fields were bare.

Jancis sat high on the last waggon, surrounded by children waving branches and wild flowers. Gideon walked along beside the waggon, tall and handsome.

In the rickyard, when the last rick had been made, Parson blessed the corn.

'Thank you kindly, friends,' said Gideon, 'for bringing the harvest home. I will do the same for every man here in return.'

A love-carriage always ends with a feast. So now everyone sat at tables in our orchard to eat and drink.

In the middle of the feast, the young squire and his sister, Miss Dorabella, rode through our gate.

'Good evening, everybody,' young Camperdine called, 'and good luck to the corn!'

'Well, Sarn,' Miss Dorabella said. 'Aren't you going to give us some harvest ale?'

Gideon poured out some ale for Dorabella and the young squire.

'I thought Beguildy would be here,' said Camperdine, 'but I don't see him.'

'No, sir,' Missis Beguildy said quickly. 'He's away for two or three weeks.'

'Right,' called the young squire. 'I'll come back then. And make sure that Venus is there too!'

Jancis laughed and I tried to hide myself so that young Camperdine would not see me. That made Jancis laugh even more.

Missis Beguildy had made a plan to get Beguildy far away at the

Ah, what a day that was! Every armful of corn was like pure gold.

time of the wedding. She had made the plan with her cousin. This cousin had asked Beguildy to bring her a special charm. She had said that she would pay Beguildy a lot of money for this charm. The charm was made with a loaf of bread baked by the seventh child of a seventh child. So Beguildy had to search all over the country to find such a child. And by the time Beguildy came back, Gideon and Jancis would be married.

It was getting late now and the moon was rising, big and round. Some men began whistling and the dancing started.

Gideon danced with Jancis and held her close.

Kester found me. 'Not dancing?' he asked.

'No.'

'Why not?' Kester asked.

'I'm not like other girls.'

Kester thought a bit and then he said, 'I must be going now. As you know, I'm off to London for ten months, to learn coloured weaving. That pays well. So next year, I'll have my own loom and work at home.'

I felt as though I was drowning.

'When will you be back?' I asked.

'I'll be back here for next August Fair[3]. I'll come and talk to you then, Prue Sarn.'

'Maybe you'll forget.'

'I don't think so,' he said.

'Well, God bless you,' I whispered.

'And you.'

'It's silly that a girl who looks like Venus does not dance.' And away he went, before I understood what his words meant.

By now, Mother was tired and ready for bed. I helped her get into bed and then stood at the bedroom window, looking down at the people.

As Gideon and Jancis walked slowly by, I heard Gideon say, 'Now your Father's away, Jancis, I'll come and stay with you at Plash tomorrow night.'

So that was his plan. Perhaps there was nothing wrong in this. After all, they were to be married in two weeks.

By the time everyone had gone and all was cleared away, it was nearly dawn. I went up to the attic and wrote in my book all that had happened. The last words I wrote were: *A girl who looks like Venus.* I felt great joy in my heart for it seemed that Kester was not troubled about my hare-lip at all.

It was a lovely fresh morning. As I went to the milking shed to milk the cows, I looked at our ricks and thanked God for such a wonderful harvest.

But suddenly the words 'precious bane' came into my mind. I felt afraid. Surely a good harvest would bring us joy, not a curse?

11

Fire!

The next day after supper, Gideon said, 'I'm going to Plash tonight, Prue. I'll be late so don't lock the door.'

I watched him as he shaved carefully and put on his best coat. He set off for Plash, whistling happily.

The wedding was going to take place in two weeks' time and the late roses were in flower. Why then did I feel so sad, so afraid?

Every evening, Gideon went to Plash and stayed there till morning. All day, he whistled as he worked.

I had prepared a bedroom for Jancis and Gideon to have when they were married. I put pretty paper all covered with roses on the walls.

Then one morning, five days before the wedding, Missis Beguildy rushed into our house like a mad woman.

'Oh, my dear!' Missis Beguildy cried, 'the worst has happened! He's come back!'

'Who? Not Mister Beguildy?'

'Yes. Someone told him about Gideon. I thought that there was nothing wrong in the lad staying all night as the wedding's so near. So I gave him and Jancis our room and I slept in the kitchen.

'Then last night, just as I was going to bed, in came Beguildy. "Well, Missis," he said, "where's Jancis?"

' "She's asleep," I said.

'Beguildy looked at me and rushed upstairs. And there they were! Beguildy put a terrible curse on Gideon and shouted, "I curse you again, by fire and water. You'll never have her now!"

'And Gideon just laughed and said, "It seems to me I've got your girl already."

'With that, Beguildy went mad with rage and picked up his old gun. I screamed and Jancis screamed. Then Gideon knocked Beguildy down and he lay on the floor without moving.

' "Take his feet, Mother Beguildy," Gideon said, "and we'll put him in the kitchen. I don't care whether he's dead or alive. I'll not be disturbed again tonight."

'Your brother's a terrible man when he's angry, Prue,' Missis Beguildy said.

'What happened to Beguildy?' I asked.

'I tied him down and then threw water over him. Then I gave him brandy till he fell asleep.

'After your brother had left this morning, I untied Beguildy,' Missis Beguildy went on, 'and he went out very quiet. That's why I ran to tell you. When Beguildy's quiet, he's to be feared.'

And Missis Beguildy ran back to Plash, wishing that the wedding day had already come.

That day, a strong wind began to blow. But Gideon said our ricks were well-made and safe. In two days a man would come to price the corn. Three days after that, Gideon and Jancis would be married.

I woke up suddenly that night. There was a bright red light

everywhere. And I heard a great roaring sound. Gideon rushed past my door, shouting for me and Mother to get up.

I ran downstairs and into the yard. And then I saw the reason for the red light and the roaring noise. Our corn, our future, was burning away before our eyes!

Oh, God, the corn! All we had and all our hope. I held onto the gate and the hot, fierce wind blew onto my face.

The wind was blowing the fire from rick to rick. As the fire grew stronger, each rick burnt white, then red, with a terrible glow.

Gideon and Sexton's family, who lived nearby, were already in the yard. Together, we stood in a line and passed bucket after bucket of water from our well. But there were too few of us. The fire had taken too strong a hold.

Only at dawn, when the wind had dropped and the rain began to fall – too late – did the fire burn itself out. Thank God, the house and animals were saved.

But the rickyard was full of black ash. And only then did we learn the cause of the fire.

'Tivvy and me were coming home late,' said Sammy, Sexton's son. 'We saw Beguildy walking towards Sarn. So we followed him, for he's such a wicked old man.

'Then we saw a great blaze of fire from the rickyard. Beguildy ran away past us, and when we got to the yard we found this – '

And Sammy held up the lid of a tinder-box[4], with Beguildy's name on it.

'Beguildy?' Gideon said in a terrible voice. 'I'll find the man and burn him, as he's burnt my corn!'

'It's the curse!' Mother cried. 'Beguildy cursed my son by fire and water. My son, the Sin Eater, is cursed!'

Gideon looked around. His face was as grey and lined as an old man's.

Then all of a sudden, he moved towards the stable. I knew what he was going to do, so I ran after him.

Our corn, our future, was burning away before our eyes!

'Gideon!' I cried. 'Help me with the cows first and go to Plash later.'

It was long past milking-time and Gideon went to the milking shed at once.

'Take Bendigo and ride to Plash,' I said quickly to Sexton and Sammy. 'Take Beguildy to Lullingford and get him locked up. The law must punish him, not Gideon.'

When Gideon heard the sound of a horse leaving the yard, he came running out of the milking-shed.

'They're going to take Beguildy to prison,' I said. 'You don't want murder on your soul, Gideon.'

'His death would have pleased me,' Gideon answered, with a strange look on his face. 'The pain of this night will never leave me now.'

'But you couldn't kill the father of your wife-to-be,' I said.

'Wife? What wife?'

'Why, Jancis, of course!'

'Never!' Gideon cried out in a terrible voice. 'Marry the Devil's daughter? No, I'll never look at the girl again.'

'Gideon, Gideon!' I cried. 'Surely your heart's not as hard as that?'

'Hard? It's like stone,' Gideon answered. 'The young squire can have her now and welcome. Jancis is as rotten as her father – rotten, rotten!'

'But suppose there is a baby?' I asked.

'My child and hers? I'd strangle it,' Gideon said. 'And I'll make sure Beguildy is hanged for what he's done to me.'

I said no more. I was frightened. I left Gideon standing like a man of stone.

Later, I found Gideon in the rickyard, lying upon his face in the ash. He was as still and deaf as a dead man. Indeed, I think Gideon's heart was dead from that time on.

12

Cursed

It was hard, very hard, for me to write down what happened next. It was a terrible time – a time of great sadness.

For many days after the fire we did no work on the farm. Each day, Gideon waited to hear of Beguildy's death. But the old man was still in prison in Silverton, waiting to be tried in court.

Missis Beguildy and Jancis were made to leave their house and they went to Silverton to be near Beguildy. They went in a waggon, for Jancis had become ill and could not walk or ride.

Gideon stood in our woods and watched the waggon go by. I saw him raise his two fists and shake them at the Beguildys.

We are all cursed, I whispered to myself.

The next morning, Gideon took the plough out of the shed.

'Come and start ploughing the big field, Prue,' he said.

'Oh, all that ploughing!' Mother said. 'But no corn, no wedding, nothing! I'm not well, Prue. Maybe I won't live to see the corn grow again. And my son doesn't love me. I'm no use on the farm. Sarn would rather I was dead!'

After that, I got Tivvy, Sexton's daughter, to sit with Mother while Gideon and I were in the fields.

Tivvy was careless and lazy, but we got her to do a little work. She did it without wages because she had always wanted Gideon. But we had to feed Tivvy and we were poorer than we had ever been.

At Christmas, a little packet was left for me at the inn in Lullingford. Inside, was a piece of cloth and a letter from Kester:

London Town
Christmas

Dear Prue Sarn,

This is to wish you well, as I am too. As you see, I can weave in two colours now. The women here are mostly small and fair. None of them has lovely dark eyes. When I look at them, I remember a small room and the young squire looking at a tall, slender woman. She did what she did for a friend. It was a hard thing for her to do. But to another man there, she looked like Venus herself. And he knows he will never forget her.

And so a happy Christmas, and a good New Year from,
Kester Woodseaves

I sat down and wrote a letter in reply:

Sarn
Christmas

Dear Weaver,

I'm sending with this letter, a shirt I sewed myself. I've said some good charms over it. If you wear it, it will keep you in good health.

I often remember the day when the water-lilies were in bloom and we watched the dragon-flies dance over the water.

So farewell for now and God make you happy.
Yours obediently,
Prudence Sarn

In January, the snow fell heavily. Mother was so ill one night, that I sent for the doctor's man[4]. He looked at Mother carefully as she lay in bed and then came downstairs. 'The old lady will live some time yet,' the doctor's man said cheerfully, as he sat by the fire.

'How many years?' Gideon asked quickly.

'Oh, it's hard to say. Perhaps ten. With care.'

'Ten years!' Gideon said, in a very strange way.

'Oh yes. As long as you give her medicine to keep her strong. She must stay in bed in winter, of course. Later on, perhaps, she'll stay in bed all the time.'

So she'll never work again, Gideon said to himself.

The weather was so bad that the doctor's man had to stay for a few days. Before he left, Gideon asked him about our old cow.

'Our old cow's got a fever,' he said. 'Her heart's beating fast. Would a dose of foxglove⁴ put her right?'

'Oh yes,' the man answered. 'Foxglove will stop the heart beating fast. But don't give her too much. It will kill her.'

From that time on, Gideon asked Mother about her health every day. He spoke in a loud voice and this frightened Mother.

'What a terrible cough you have, Mother,' he said. 'You must be in pain. I'm sure you'd rather be dead than alive, Mother.'

'Well, maybe I would, Sarn,' she answered sadly one day.

This answer seemed to please Gideon.

One day, in early April, when I was in the fields sowing corn, Tivvy came up shouting, 'Come quick, Prue. Your mother's very ill. Gideon told me to make the tea strong. She drank it and then went very quiet. "Get Prue!" she said.'

I ran back to the house. As I bent over to kiss Mother, she whispered, 'The tea was so bitter.' Then she died.

'Gideon!' I cried out. 'What was in that tea?'

'What do I know about the tea?' Gideon said.

'Oh, Sarn,' Tivvy said. 'You know you told me to make it strong and to be sure your mother drank it all.'

'Be quiet, you little liar!' Gideon shouted. 'Or I'll make you tell Prue what you and I were doing in the loft last Sunday!'

Tivvy's face became red and she said nothing more.

So I sent for the doctor. I wanted to find out why Mother had died. The doctor asked if we'd ever given Mother foxglove.

'Foxglove? What should we give her that for?' I asked in surprise. 'Just tell me how she died.'

'I'd like to know that myself,' the doctor replied.

'Maybe we should have an inquest[4], sir,' I said.

'Are you ready to have an inquest?' the doctor asked slowly.

'Why, yes sir.'

'Well, I'm not sure if we need an inquest,' said the doctor. 'An inquest costs a lot of money. And it doesn't help the person who is dead. And the fact that you are ready to have an inquest shows that we don't need one. No, I don't think we'll have an inquest.'

At that time, I did not understand at all what the doctor meant. But later, to my great horror and sadness I came to understand.

———

Now it was quieter than ever at Sarn. I missed Mother a lot and often cried for her in the evenings.

Work went on and we had goods to take to market again.

Either Gideon or I would go to Lullingford.

When Gideon went, Miss Dorabella always bought something from him, for she wanted him, just as Tivvy did.

Gideon cared nothing for Tivvy, I knew. But he was ready to take all she gave. And he stayed near her too, when he wasn't working.

Gideon never spoke about Mother, but sometimes he'd look at her empty chair in a strange way. And sometimes, when all was quiet, he seemed to be listening for something.

May came and the colours of the trees and flowers made me think of Kester and his coloured weaving.

We were having dinner in the kitchen one day, when something went past the window. I heard a soft tap at the door. When I opened it, there stood Jancis.

She was wearing a white dress and her face was as white as a ghost. And wrapped in a shawl, she carried a baby no bigger than a doll.

'Why, Jancis!' I cried. 'How did you get here?'

Jancis, all in white, moved across the kitchen without speaking. She laid the baby on the floor at Gideon's feet. Then she knelt down beside it.

The sun shone on her golden hair and she was all white and gold.

Tears ran down my face, for Jancis and her baby looked so pale and ill. Tivvy sat with her mouth open, but Gideon showed no feeling at all.

'Sarn,' Jancis whispered. 'Sarn, look at me. Don't you remember the sweet times we had together? How you kissed me in the dairy and how we danced together at the harvest? And how you said, "Soon we'll be married, my little dear." Do you remember, Sarn?'

'It was all long ago,' Gideon said, his face hard.

'Sarn, this is our baby. Yours and mine.'

Jancis held up the child, but Gideon turned away.

'It's a boy,' Jancis said, 'a boy to help you with the farm. He'll be a good lad and work hard, I know.'

Gideon looked at the baby and gave a hard laugh.

'That?' he said. 'You offer me that poor thing to help me? Why, I don't think it will live.'

The baby started to cry, as if it understood what its father had said.

Gideon stood up and walked towards the door.

'Go back to where you came from,' he said. 'You're not wanted here – neither you nor the baby.' And he walked out, shutting the door behind him.

Jancis knelt on the floor without a word. I ran to her and made her sit down on the settle. I gave her tea and, as she drank it, the tears ran down her pale face.

'I walked here from Silverton, Prue,' Jancis whispered.

'What was your mother thinking of?' I cried.

'Mother's dead.'

'Dear me. I'm sorry for that. Then your home's here with us, Jancis, my dear.'

'But it cannot be, if Gideon doesn't love me.'

'While I am here, you are welcome to stay,' I said.

Then Tivvy jumped up and shouted, 'Is she indeed, Prue Sarn? I don't think so. For Sarn's going to marry me. He's got to.'

'Go back to where you came from. You're not wanted here –
neither you nor the baby.'

'It would be better for you if he did,' I said, looking hard at Tivvy, for she was going to have a child. 'But will he?'

'Sarn had better marry me,' Tivvy said. 'And I'll tell you why. Foxglove tea, that's why!'

'What do you mean, Tivvy?' I cried.

'There were foxglove leaves in the tea your mother drank. Gideon told me to make it strong.' Then Tivvy turned to Jancis and said, 'If you stay here one night, Jancis Beguildy, I'll tell everyone what Gideon did.'

Then I lost my temper. I ran at Tivvy and struck her face and shouted, 'Go! Get out of this house before I make you. How can you be so cruel to this poor child! You and Gideon may do what you like. When you come here to live, I'll go. But for today, you're going out – now!'

And Tivvy was so surprised that she ran out without saying a word.

'Now you rest here on the settle, Jancis,' I said. 'You and the child.'

'Thank you, Prue,' she whispered.

I went straight out and found Gideon.

'Tivvy says you gave Mother foxglove leaves to kill her. Is that true?'

'My God, that girl wants a good beating!' Gideon said.

'Perhaps,' I answered. 'But you made sure Mother drank the tea, didn't you?'

'Mother told me she'd rather be dead than alive. And she could not work on the farm any more.'

'Then you are a murderer and I've finished with you.'

'You promised to do all I said!' Gideon shouted.

'Murder changes everything,' I told him. 'You'll have Tivvy.'

'I don't want Tivvy. She's lazy and she doesn't want to work.'

'You either have Tivvy or you hang,' I said. 'You're my brother and I cannot hate you. But why did you do such a thing? You murdered your own mother, Gideon!'

'She could not work any more,' Gideon said again. 'You must stay till after the harvest, Prue.'

'No, I'll stay till Tivvy comes here as your wife. That must be soon. But what about Jancis and that poor child, your own son?'

For answer, Gideon looked across at the rickyard and said, 'You know whose child Jancis is.' Then quietly to himself he said, 'But I did love her once.'

So I left him to his thoughts and ran back to the house.

But the kitchen was empty.

I ran out to the road and looked up and down. I ran round the first corner and the next. But she wasn't there. Then I ran back to the house and into every room, calling, 'Jancis, Jancis.'

I ran outside again, calling, calling and the smell of flowers was sweet on the air.

At last I ran back to Gideon and said, 'I can't find Jancis anywhere.'

'I told her to go back where she came from,' he said.

'She can't do that. She's got no money and her mother's dead. Her father's in prison and no one knows what will happen to him. She walked all the way from Silverton, Gideon, miles and miles. And you turned her away!'

Gideon said nothing, but went on working.

'You must help me find her now,' I said. 'I've looked and looked everywhere. There's only . . .'

And I pointed to the Mere.

'What? You want to frighten me, do you?' Gideon shouted.

But he came with me to the Mere.

And on the path leading to the water, I saw one of the baby's shoes. In the water, Jancis and the baby lay dead – drowned among the lilies. Without a word, Gideon and I lifted them out of the water and carried them into the house.

I washed them, dressed them in clean, white clothes and lay them on Mother's bed. Then I covered the bed with flowers – white and gold like poor Jancis herself.

73

People came from far and near to look at Jancis and her dead child.

Women cried and men looked at the beautiful dead girl with pity.

All this time, Gideon said nothing. But the night we took them to the churchyard, I heard him go to the room where Jancis lay.

Gideon stood there quietly. Then very gently, he touched Jancis's hair and whispered, 'I did love her once.'

13

Ghosts

Now comes the most terrible part of my story. It is difficult for me to tell, but I must try. The truth must be told.

Gideon had always been a quiet man, but from that time on he never spoke a word.

Tivvy wanted to marry Gideon, but she was frightened to live at Sarn. So I stayed and helped with the work.

Then it was July and the weather got very hot. One day, I was sitting in the doorway, spinning yarn. Suddenly Gideon came round the corner, all hot and covered with sweat.

'Why are you sitting there looking like Mother?' he shouted. 'Mother used to sit there and spin yarn. I thought you were Mother.'

'But you can see I'm not Mother,' I said. 'And why did you rush round the corner so quickly?'

'I was cutting the hedge[3] and I saw her on top of it, all in white.'

'Who?' I asked.

'Jancis,' Gideon replied.

The next time he saw Jancis, she was ploughing with two white oxen, with the child sitting on one of them.

'Now look, Gideon,' I said. 'You must stop thinking of Jancis, or you'll go mad.'

'I don't think of her,' Gideon said. 'She just comes.'

'Well, try to think of other things,' I said. 'Working hard, getting rich, buying the house.'

'I don't want it.'

'Why not? You wanted it so much you poisoned Mother and sent Jancis away.'

'But I don't want it now. Everything changed when I saw them in the water.'

'Well, think of Tivvy. Or Miss Dorabella. She wants you, doesn't she?'

'Dorabella's a dark woman. I like a fair woman with blue eyes.'

'Well, think of me then. I'll stay here with you for a while longer. But you must be happier and stop thinking of the past.'

But I was not able to help him. After a few days, he saw Jancis again. And many times after that.

'I saw her in the wood today,' Gideon would say. Or, 'There she is, on the path. She's coming up from the Mere, all wet.' And once, he saw Jancis standing in a boat in the middle of the Mere.

And then, at the beginning of August, Gideon heard Jancis singing across the water.

'And the sound comes into the house,' he said.

I closed the window, but Gideon said he could still hear her singing.

Then it was the middle of August and time for the August Fair at Sarn Mere. People were getting ready for the fair on the meadow between the church and the Mere.

Miss Dorabella sent a letter and I read it to Gideon. It said that Beguildy would only stay in prison for a short time because of what had happened to his daughter.

'Damn. I hoped he would hang,' Gideon said, and his eyes blazed with hate. But soon after, he became sad again. This time, it was Mother he saw in the woods.

'Yes, Prue,' he said. 'It was Mother. I see them both now – Mother and Jancis.'

We sat quiet a little and then he whispered, 'Listen! There's Jancis singing again!'

Gideon held up his hand and began to sing the song that Jancis had loved. He sat watching the open door.

'Here's Jancis,' he said, 'all wet from the Mere. Look, her gown's all wet with water.' And he sat there for a long time, gazing at the floor.

Later, Gideon stood up and said he was going to look at the animals. He looked so strange that I almost went after him. But I stayed where I was, reading, for about half an hour.

At about nine o'clock, there was a knocking at the door and in rushed Sammy, Sexton's son.

'Oh, Prue, Prue. I've just seen Sarn standing near the Mere. He was walking down the path, like someone asleep. He got into the boat and went straight out into the middle of the Mere.'

I ran out of the house and down the path to the water. I saw the boat in the water, but it was empty.

So the Mere became Gideon's grave. My brother had been a strong man and a hard one. He had done wrong to those who loved him. But he paid for all by his death.

14

The August Fair

That was a night of such horror and sadness that I shall never forget it. I sat alone, hour after hour, saying prayers for the dead. I thought of how Beguildy had cursed Gideon by fire and by water. I thought of those who had died – golden Jancis, her baby, Missis Beguildy, Father and poor Mother.

I remembered happy times, too, when Gideon and Jancis had played together as children and all the happiness they had shared since that time.

I knew I could not spend another night at the farm alone. I knew no one would stay there with me. Everybody was afraid of the ghosts that haunted the place. I had to leave. But what could I do with the animals?

Dawn came and I remembered that this was the day of the August Fair. There'd be lots of people there. I decided to feed the animals, drive them to the fair and sell them.

There was no time to waste. I walked along by the Mere to the meadow where the people were starting to arrive.

I saw Mister Huglet and Mister Grimble and they both looked angrily at me as I went by.

All along the Mere, I saw the dragon-flies flying over the water. I thought of Kester Woodseaves. I was sure he had forgotten me.

When I'd arranged for the animals to be sold, I went back home again. I gathered all the animals together. Riding our old horse, Bendigo, I drove them to the fair.

Then I went back for the birds, put them in baskets and took them to the fair too. Last of all, I put the cat in a basket and locked the door of the house behind me.

So I left the farm. The only things I took with me were my Bible and my book. It was hard to leave. But I knew I could not stay.

The animals were being sold when I got back to the fair. I sat on the churchyard wall and waited.

I gave the cat to Felena, the shepherd's wife. She asked about Kester and I told her that I had not heard of him for a long time.

So I sat on the churchyard wall, very sad, and the people walked by me. They gave me looks of hate, black hate, which hurt me terribly. I began to grow afraid, for there were at least three hundred people at the fair. But I had to wait for the money I would get for the animals.

Someone told me that Grimble and Huglet had been telling

stories about me. They were saying that I was a witch and that Beguildy had cursed the farm. Then Mother had died, Jancis and lastly, Gideon.

As I was the one left alive, people were saying that I was the reason for all these things. Was I not cursed with the Devil's mark, a hare-lip? Was I not the witch of Sarn who had been taught by that wicked old man, Beguildy himself?

While I was thinking about all this, Tivvy ran up to me and said, 'You struck my face, Prue Sarn. Now see what I'll do.' With that, she jumped up on the wall and shouted, 'People, listen to me. I'm a wronged woman. Sarn promised to marry me five months ago and Prue Sarn stopped it. She stopped it and made me afraid for my life. She is a witch and she wanted to be the only woman on the farm. And the day after my Sarn's death, she sells everything. I would have been Missis Sarn, but for her!'

Then Grimble began to speak.

'People,' he said, 'this is a sad day. A fine farmer lies drowned in the water. And he was going to marry a good woman.

'Now, listen. Prudence Sarn is a woman cursed from birth. We know she runs through the fields like a hare. You all know what she did to my dog.

'But there's worse yet. How did her mother die? She died of foxglove tea. Poisoned. And who looks after a sick mother? Why, her daughter. Well, people, what do you say to that?'

The crowd came nearer to me and I was filled with terror. But Grimble hadn't finished.

'Who was alone in the house when Jancis Beguildy and her child went to their deaths in the water? Why, Prudence Sarn! Why did the witch hate Jancis? Because Jancis knew that old Beguildy had taught Prue Sarn to be a witch.

'And the witch murdered her brother too. She did not want to see him married. Yes, friends, she pushed him in the water.'

Grimble waited for a moment and then he said, 'Cursed by God! A witch! Three times a murderess!'

And Huglet roared out, 'A witch, she must not live!'

'Kill her! Kill her! Let the witch drown!'

Rough hands took hold of me. Some people ran to the church for the ducking-stool[2].

'A witch! A witch!' they cried out. 'She must not live!'

I fainted. The next thing I knew I was tied with rope to the ducking-stool and I was in the cold water of the Mere.

Then I was out of the water and able to open my eyes. I looked up and thought I was dead and in heaven.

There, looking down at me from his old white horse, was Kester Woodseaves!

His blue eyes looked down at me. He looked at me from head to foot. I was at rest. Yes, even though I was tied to the ducking-stool, I was at rest, for Kester was there.

Who could harm me now? Though three hundred were against me, Kester was here and I knew I was safe.

'Well, Prue, my dear,' he said at last, 'you're in a bad way.' And he smiled at me.

My voice shook with happiness as I said, 'I'm in a very bad way, Kester Woodseaves.'

Kester looked round and said to the shepherd's wife, Felena, 'Untie those ropes, will you?' And Felena ran forward to do it.

'Is there any man here who would hold my horse for a moment?' Kester asked.

Callard, who owned the white bull, called out, 'Yes, I will and welcome.'

Kester looked at all the people.

'Well, you were all having a fine time, I must say. Last time, you were baiting a white bull. Now it's a woman, whiter than a lily.'

Kester went up to Grimble.

'Your nose is too long, Grimble,' Kester said. And with that, Kester hit Grimble so hard on the nose that he roared with pain.

Then Kester went up to Huglet.

'Will you wrestle with me?' he asked.

79

I looked up and thought I was dead and in heaven! There, looking down at me from his old white horse, was Kester Woodseaves!

Now Huglet knew that Kester was a good wrestler, so he said nothing. But all the people cried out, 'Let's have some wrestling!'

'Stand round! Make a circle!' someone called out.

'Right, men, there's a nice piece of grass near the water,' Kester said. So they made a circle there.

Kester took off his coat and so did Huglet. But I saw that Huglet didn't want to wrestle.

Huglet was full of hate and did his best to break Kester's back, but Kester was a very good wrestler.

All this time, Kester had been moving nearer the water. I wondered why, for the ground was very muddy there. Then suddenly, Kester gave a twist and Huglet was in the Mere. Huglet climbed out covered with mud. Everyone shouted with laughter.

Kester stood for a minute. Then he took the reins of his horse and jumped up into the saddle.

'Prue!' he called.

I stood up.

'Did I say at the harvest, that you should come nearer to me or draw back?'

'Come nearer,' I whispered.

'Come here, then, Prue Woodseaves!'

He leant over, put his strong arms round me and lifted me into the saddle. And suddenly, everything was quiet.

'On you go, old horse,' Kester said and we were on our way to the high, blue mountains.

'Wait,' I said. 'I must draw back. You must marry a girl like a lily. You cannot marry me. I am cursed with a hare-lip.'

Kester stopped the horse.

'No more sad talk, Prue,' he said. 'I have my heaven here on earth. And it's here, near your heart, my dearest love.'

And then he bent down his head and kissed me on my mouth.

Here ends the story of Prudence Sarn.

Points for Understanding

Introduction

1 Why does the writer want to write down her story?
2 Does the writer think Mister Beguildy was a wicked man?

1

1 Why did Prue Sarn's mother often cry when she looked at her daughter?
2 What was the cause of Sarn's death?
3 Who was the chief mourner at Sarn's funeral?
4 'I'll be the Sin Eater,' Gideon said. What did Gideon make his mother promise to give him?
5 Why were the people afraid of Missis Beguildy's husband?

2

1 Outline the plans which Gideon was making for the future. What part did Gideon want Prue to play in his plans? Did Prue want the same things in life as Gideon?
2 Why did Gideon think Prue would never marry?
3 What did Gideon promise to give Prue when he had made enough money and sold the farm?
4 'Mister Beguildy? What for?' I asked in surprise.
   (a) Why was Prue surprised when Gideon asked her to go to visit Beguildy?
   (b) What was Prue to do there?
   (c) How was Prue to pay Beguildy?
5 'Was it my fault?' Prue's mother asked. What was she talking about?
6 How was Prue able to get away from Gideon and the work on the farm?

3

1 What two pieces of news did they hear in the year 1815? What news changed their lives most? How did it change their lives?
2 Did Gideon love the farm in the same way Prue did?

3 What was Gideon going to do with the money Prue made picking up the leasings in Beguildy's fields?
4 Missis Beguildy loved to see Gideon and Jancis together.
  (a) Was Mister Beguildy happy to see Gideon in his house?
  (b) What tricks did Missis Beguildy use to get her husband out of the house?
  (c) Did Prue think that Gideon really loved Jancis?
5 Who was Tivvy? Why was she jealous of Jancis?
6 Why did Prue notice the weaver's cottage in Lullingford?
7 Why did the men in the inn stop singing when they saw Prue? What did one old man say to another?
8 Why did Miss Dorabella speak about broomsticks and ask Gideon if he was going to go dancing on the mountainside? What was Gideon's reply?
9 'Now, Prue,' Gideon said, 'you must know how I feel about Jancis.'
  (a) Describe the house which Gideon showed to Prue.
  (b) Was Gideon ready to give up his plans in order to marry Jancis?
  (c) Who did Gideon say he might marry?
  (d) What was Gideon's final decision?

4

1 Why was Beguildy not a happy man?
2 What advice did Prue give to Beguildy?
3 Who did Prue meet at the love-spinning? What words did she write in her book?

5

1 What bet had Beguildy made with the squire's son?
2 What did Jancis have to do with the bet? Why was she afraid to do it?
3 Who took Jancis' place?
4 How was the trick done?
5 Who saw Prue?
6 Why would Gideon grow nothing but corn?
7 Why was Prue suddenly made happy by her mother's words?
8 What was Beguildy going to do if Jancis didn't agree to go with the squire's son?
9 What did Gideon say when Jancis asked him to marry her immediately?
10 What did Prue think might become their 'precious bane'?

6

1 What did Gideon ask Prue to do for him?
2 Why did Beguildy curse Gideon? How did he curse him?
3 Prue thanked the weaver in her heart for some words he spoke. What were the words?
4 What did Prue think was a sad thing?

7

1 'I want to stop baiting all over England,' the weaver answered.
    (a) Why did the weaver want to stop baiting?
    (b) Did the farmers agree with him?
    (c) What did the weaver offer to give Mister Callard?
2 'We want our sport,' Huglet shouted.
    (a) What did Kester offer to do with each one of them?
    (b) Why did none of the farmers accept his offer?
    (c) What did Kester agree to do?
3 Describe how Prue saved Kester's life.
4 What did Prue's mother say when Prue told her what had happened?

8

1 How did Prue's mother trick Prue into telling her that she loved the weaver?
2 How was Prue able to tell Kester that she loved him? What was Kester able to reply?
3 Why did Jancis run away from Grimble's farm?
4 Why did Prue write another letter to Kester? What did she say in this letter?
5 Where did Prue help Jancis to get another job?
6 What did Beguildy say when Prue told him Gideon was going to marry Jancis in the autumn?
7 Why did Jancis tell Prue she was going to send for the weaver soon?

9

1 How did Gideon look at the golden corn?
2 How did Kester find out that it was Prue's own words she put in the letters?
3 What did Kester say Prue could write in her book?

10

1 Why was Gideon going to be a rich man? What was Prue going to do with the money Gideon had promised to give her?
2 Why did Kester use the words 'You are safe now' when speaking to Prue?
3 How was Missis Beguildy planning to get her husband far away at the time of the wedding?
4 Kester was going to London.
    (a) How long was he going to stay there?
    (b) What was he going to do there?
5 What was Gideon planning to do while Jancis' father was away?
6 What words did Prue write in her book?
7 What words came into Prue's mind as she looked at the golden harvest?

11

1 What happened the night Beguildy came back?
2 What had Beguildy left near the ricks which proved that he had set the ricks on fire?
3 How did Prue stop Gideon killing Beguildy?
4 Why would Gideon not marry Jancis?
5 'But suppose there is a baby?' I asked. What was Gideon's reply?

12

1 Why did Prue get Tivvy to sit with Mother? Why did Tivvy do it without wages?
2 What did Kester remember when he looked at the women in London? What day did Prue often think of?

3 Prue sent for the doctor's man.
   (a) Why did she send for him?
   (b) How long did he say their mother would live?
   (c) What did Gideon say when he heard this?
4 Why did Gideon want to give the sick cow foxglove?
5 What did Mother whisper to Prue before she died?
6 '. . . the fact that you are ready to have an inquest shows that we
   don't need one,' said the doctor. Why was Prue full of horror when
   she at last understood these words of the doctor?
7 What did Gideon say to Jancis when he saw her with the baby?
8 What did Tivvy say she would do if Gideon didn't marry her? Why
   did Prue say her promise to Gideon was at an end?
9 How did Jancis and the baby die?

13

1 Why did Prue stay at Sarn?
2 What kind of things did Gideon begin to see?
3 When did Gideon stop wanting to get rich?
4 What kind of things did Gideon begin to hear?
5 Why would Beguildy not be hanged?
6 How did Gideon die?

14

1 Why would no one stay with Prue at the farm?
2 Why did Prue decide to drive the animals to the August Fair?
3 Who did Prue think had forgotten her?
4 Why did Prue begin to feel afraid?
5 What did Tivvy tell everybody? Did the people believe her?
6 What crimes did Farmer Grimble say Prue was guilty of?
7 Why did the people tie Prue to the ducking-stool?
8 How did Kester save Prue?
9 How did Kester show that he really loved Prue?

Glossary

SECTION 1

Some examples of old-fashioned English

The English in this story has been modernised where necessary. But a few examples of old-fashioned English and special words used in the country have been kept. A few are listed here and others, for example ducking-stool, are listed in the Sections below.

aye (page 23)
> a word meaning 'yes'. Here Sarn uses the word to show he is very determined.

learning (page 5)
> an older word for the modern word – education.

Mere – *Sarn Mere* (page 5)
> the name of the lake beside Sarn's Farm. The word mere is seen in the names of many lakes in England. For example, Lake Windermere.

SECTION 2

Terms to do with magic and common beliefs

At the time of this story, country people still believed strongly in many things that we no longer believe in in the same way today. For example, it was commonly believed you could do harm to a person by using magic.

angel – *guardian angel* (page 44)
> Prue Sarn believed that everybody had a good spirit who took care of them. On that day she was the weaver's guardian angel.

away – *tell the bees or they'll fly away* (page 7)
> there were many strange beliefs about bees. When the head of a family died, the eldest son or daughter had to go and tell the bees and ask the bees to accept them as their new master. If the bees were not told, they would all fly away.

Beguildy – *Wizard Beguildy* (page 6)

a wizard was a magician. Everyone thought that Beguildy was a magician so they called him Wizard Beguildy.

curse (page 5)

to curse a person is to use magic words so that bad things happen to that person.

ducking-stool (page 79)

the ducking-stool was used to find out if a woman was a witch. The woman was tied to the stool which was placed over deep water. When the stool was lowered into the water, the woman's head went under the water. If the woman did not drown, then the Devil must be helping her so she must be a witch. If she was a witch, she must be put to death. If the woman drowned, she was not a witch, but it was too late to help her. (See the illustration on pages 80–81)

Eater – *Sin Eater* (page 8)

a Sin Eater was a poor man who was paid to be responsible for a dead person's sins by eating bread and drinking wine at the funeral. In the life that came after death, it was the Sin Eater who would be punished for the sins of the dead person.

fairy (page 14)

people believed in fairies. These were small, beautiful people who lived in woods and sometimes visited people's homes at night.

hell-fire (page 6)

Hell is a place where bad people go after they die. They are punished in Hell by being thrown into huge fires where they burn for ever.

lip – *hare-lip* (page 6)

Prue Sarn, the heroine in this story, was born with a hare-lip. This is a split in the upper lip through which the teeth can sometimes be seen. People thought that babies were born with hare-lips if a pregnant woman saw a hare – an animal like a rabbit – before the child was born. People with hare-lips were often thought to be witches or servants of the Devil.

peace – *drink to the peace* (page 7)

as each mourner takes a drink of wine, they pray that the dead person will rest in peace and not be punished in Hell.

Venus – *call up Venus* (page 30)

Venus was the Roman goddess of love. It was believed that magicians could call Venus and make her appear in the shape of a beautiful young woman.

SECTION 3

Terms to do with farming and local customs

At the time of this story, all the tools and machines described in this list were used by hand or were pulled by oxen or horses.

acre (page 12)
> a measure of land a little over four thousand square metres.

apothecary (page 44)
> a chemist who makes and sells medicines.

bull-baiting (page 38)
> a cruel sport in which a bull was chained to a post. Fierce dogs then fought the bull. It is now against the law in Britain.

chickens (page 16)
> the chickens had to be shut up safely each night or they might be eaten by foxes.

dairymaid (page 34)
> a woman who looks after the cows and milks them twice a day. She makes butter and cheese from the milk.

day – *market-day* (page 12)
> market-day is a special day in country towns when farmers come to town to sell their goods.

Fair – *Hiring Fair* (page 35)
> these are special market-days during the year. Servants and farm workers are hired – agree to work for someone for an amount of money – at the Hiring Fair. And the August Fair is special because August is the time of the harvest and everyone has a great many goods to sell.

fishing-lines (page 16)
> long lines with hooks on them which were placed in rivers or lakes to catch fish.

gentry (page 19)
> the important man in a country district was the squire. He owned much land and was also the local magistrate. The squire and his family and their friends were known as the gentry. Every year the squire would have a big party called the hunt ball.

hedge (page 74)
> a line of low trees or bushes which separates one field from the next.

leasing (page 17)
    picking up the corn that fell to the ground when the corn was being cut and gathered during the harvest.

loom (page 16)
    a loom was a hand machine which was used to make cloth. See *weaver* below.

love-spinning (page 25)
    when a wedding was arranged, it was the custom for all the farmers' wives and daughters to meet together to spin yarn. The yarn was then woven into cloth. The cloth was then made into new bedsheets for the bride and groom. See *spin* and *weaver* below.

meadow *hay-meadow* (page 13)
    a field which was kept for growing hay. Hay is dried grass which is fed to animals. Gideon uses a scythe – a long blade – to cut the hay.

milking-stool (page 37)
    a special seat for the person who milks a cow.

orchard (page 10)
    a wood where fruit trees grow.

oxen (page 7)
    heavy, large male cattle used for pulling waggons or ploughs. See *plough* below.

plough (page 12)
    the plough was pulled by oxen or horses. It had a sharp blade which cut into the ground.

ricks (page 57)
    corn was put together in bundles which were placed carefully on top of one another to make a rick. The corn in the rick was kept safe and dry until it was sold. The rickyard was the part of the farm where the ricks were built.

settle (page 18)
    a long, low seat near the fire in a country farmhouse.

sheaves – *corn sheaves* (page 57)
    corn that has been cut and dried and tied into bundles.

smithy (page 19)
    the smithy was the place where a fire was burnt to make metal red-hot so that it could be hammered into shape. Shoes for horses and many farm tools were made in the smithy.

spin (page 12)

thread – or yarn – was made by twisting and turning fibres from certain plants or wool from sheep in a spinning-wheel. The yarn was then woven into cloth by a weaver. See also *loom*, *love-spinning* and *weaver*.

sport – *spoil our sport* (page 41)

the farmers enjoyed watching the dogs fighting the bull and they thought bull-baiting was an exciting game or sport.

traps (page 16)

a metal device used to catch rabbits.

weave – *weave with colours* (page 57)

a *loom* (see above) had recently been invented which made it possible to weave different coloured threads together.

weaver (page 19)

the weaver travelled to farmhouses round the country making cloth on the looms in each farm.

woods – *keep pigs in the woods* (page 12)

every farm had a few pigs which provided meat during the winter. The pigs were kept in woods to eat leaves, roots, nuts and grass.

wrestler (page 29)

wrestling is a sport in which two men fight each other. Each man tries to throw the other man to the ground.

SECTION 4

General

accounts (page 13)

to keep accounts is to write down in a book all the money that is made on a farm and all the money that is spent.

ashamed (page 6)

to feel ashamed is to feel guilty or sorry for something you have done.

attic (page 16)

a room at the top of a house, under the roof. An attic in a farmhouse was used as a store-room.

bonnet (page 39)

a hat worn by a lady.

china (page 11)

good quality plates, cups and saucers.

Day – *Boxing Day* (page 50)
  the 26th December, the day after Christmas Day. A holiday in England.

dragon-fly (page 53)
  an insect with a thin body and two pairs of large wings.

drive (page 21)
  a broad path up to the front door of a large house.

election (page 21)
  in the nineteenth century, not many people were allowed to vote in an election. But Gideon Sarn owned the land his farm was on and so he was able to vote.

faint (page 42)
  to faint is to fall down on the ground and not know what has happened to you.

feast – *funeral feast* (page 8)
  after a person was buried, the family and friends were invited to the home for a meal.

foxglove (page 68)
  a tall, purple flower whose leaves contain a poison which can affect your heart.

hire (page 17)
  Gideon will pay the miller so he can borrow his pony for a day.

inquest (page 69)
  if a person dies and the reason for the death is not clear, an inquest is held to find out why the person died.

man – *doctor's man* (page 67)
  there were not many doctors in country districts. A doctor's man was a person who was not fully trained but he did the work of a doctor.

match (page 24)
  a wedding arrangement that was agreed between two families.

mattress (page 7)
  a long, thin, cloth bag filled with straw or feathers. You sleep on a mattress on a bed.

miser (page 53)
  a person who loves money and spends as little as possible.

mourner – *chief mourner* (page 7)
  the chief mourner was the closest relative to the dead person.

quick-tempered (page 5)
  a quick-tempered person is someone who is easily made angry.

reflected (page 5)

    the water of the lake was like a mirror and the sky could be seen shining on the surface of the water.

sermon (page 6)

    a talk given by the priest or minister in church.

Sexton (page 8)

    a church official who arranges funerals.

slender (page 17)

    thin and good-looking.

tinder-box (page 63)

    before matches were invented, people made fire by striking a piece of flint stone against metal.

trap-door (page 30)

    a door in a floor or ceiling through which you can pass things.

whore (page 23)

    a woman who sleeps with men, often for money.

Of Mice and Men *by John Steinbeck*
Bleak House *by Charles Dickens*
The Great Ponds *by Elechi Amadi*
Rebecca *by Daphne du Maurier*
Our Mutual Friend *by Charles Dickens*
The Grapes of Wrath *by John Steinbeck*
The Return of the Native *by Thomas Hardy*
Weep Not, Child *by Ngũgĩ wa Thiong'o*
Precious Bane *by Mary Webb*
Mine Boy *by Peter Abrahams*

For further information on the full selection of Readers at
all five levels in the series, please refer to the Heinemann
Guided Readers catalogue.

Heinemann International
A division of Heinemann Publishers (Oxford) Ltd
Halley Court, Jordan Hill, Oxford OX2 8EJ

OXFORD   LONDON   EDINBURGH
MADRID   ATHENS   BOLOGNA   PARIS
MELBOURNE   SYDNEY   AUCKLAND   SINGAPORE   TOKYO
IBADAN   NAIROBI   HARARE   GABORONE
PORTSMOUTH (NH)

ISBN 0 435 27260 8

This retold version for Heinemann Guided Readers
© Florence Bell 1990, 1992
First published 1990
This edition published 1992

Typography by Adrian Hodgkins
Cover by Helen Jones and Threefold Design
Typeset in 10.5/12.5 pt Goudy
by Joshua Associates Ltd, Oxford
Printed and bound in Malta

92 93 94 95 96 97 10 9 8 7 6 5 4 3 2 1